MASKED IN PARADISE

A DESTINATION DEATH MYSTERY

CHARLEY MARSH

TIMBERDOODLE PRESS

Timberdoodle Press

P.O. Box 194

Houston, MN 55943

timberdoodle@goacentek.net

Print Book ISBN# 978-1-945856-70-9

Cover Art: nordenworks.gmail.com /depositphotos.com

CHAPTER ONE

Harriet Monroe, known to most as simply Harry, stood on her lanai and looked out over the turquoise waters lapping the white sand beach at the rear of her cottage. She'd only been working at the Island Resort for six weeks but the place already felt like home. This was where she was meant to be.

A soft breeze freshened off the ocean and ruffled her honey blonde hair. The breeze smelled of salt and dried seaweed left on the beach by the receding tide.

She'd landed her dream job—public relations director for the most exclusive resort on the planet. Who'd have thought that a high school dropout could do so well for herself? Not that she'd dropped out of school by choice. It had been forced on her when she had run away from her aunt and warped uncle at the tender age of fifteen.

Harriet grinned. Warm, salt-scented air, exotic flowers, turquoise waters, an incredibly beautiful cottage all to herself—she'd come a long way from the cold New England winters of the last twenty years.

The days when she'd sought shelter in doorways and stairwells because she had nowhere else to sleep seemed to belong to another person.

Dream job, dream location. What else could she ask for from life?

"You ready to do this, Harry?" Solomon Ayers called to her as he stepped out onto the lanai of the cottage next to hers. Tall, slim, but well built with the chiseled features sculptors worked hard to recreate, all finished off with thick sable brown hair and warm brown eyes–Solly was a package that made many a girl's heart stutter.

Unfortunately for those girls, Solly's interests lay elsewhere, a fact his father hadn't been able to accept. The senior Ayers had tried beating the "sickness" out of his son until Solly decided he'd had enough and run away.

The two young teenagers had met up on the streets of Portland and had immediately connected, helping each other avoid those who preyed on young runaways.

Harriet grinned over at her best friend. "I'll meet you out front. I just need to lock up." She turned away from the view and hurried back inside the cottage, locking the double glass doors that led from her bedroom to the lanai.

A massive king-size bed surrounded by filmy white insect curtains dominated the large, mahogany-paneled room. The room felt cool and soothing after the brightness of the sun's rays bouncing off sand and water, a deliberate effect created by the island's interior designer.

Harriet had yet to meet Jan Rhymes, but when she did she intended to give the designer a big hug. Jan had done an outstanding job putting together not only Mermaid Cottage where Harriet lived, but also Harriet's new office. Both places were luxurious beyond Harriet's wildest expectations.

She hurried through the cottage and double-checked the remaining two sets of doors that opened onto the wrap-around lanai. It had only been two short weeks since she'd been attacked in her cottage, and while her brain understood that the threat no longer existed her emotions insisted that she still take precautions.

Grabbing the small canvas knapsack that served as her handbag, Harriet let herself out the front door and locked that as well. Solly watched her but said nothing about her paranoia. Solly always understood, and for that she loved her closest friend more than she could ever express.

Harriet tucked her hand inside Solly's arm and they headed up the crushed pink shell road toward the main resort. She preferred walking to her office over driving one of the resort's open carts, probably because she had the choice. Walking to work on the coast of Maine during the winter had never been an option.

"Have you tried the spa yet, Sol?" she asked.

"Nope. It wasn't finished when I first arrived, and then I got too busy with the greenhouses and grounds crews to take the time. I've heard good things about it, though."

Harriet knew that her friend loved his work. She wasn't the only one who had landed their dream job. Solly was in charge of the resort's seven greenhouses that grew the flowers for the guest cottages and the arrangements for the public areas like the dining rooms, various lobbies, and anywhere else flowers were needed–which was pretty much everywhere a guest might roam.

The greenhouses also provided the kitchen with some of the more exotic greens, fruits, and vegetables that they served to the guests. And if that wasn't enough, Solly also managed the groundskeepers who kept the resort looking pristine and otherworldly beautiful.

He did the work of three men and seemed to thrive on it, but in the last few days Harriet had noticed a slight tightening around her friend's eyes that told her he needed a break. He had confirmed her suspicion when he readily agreed to take a day off to visit the spa with her.

They walked along in a companionable silence, the road's crushed shells crunching softly under Harriet's sandaled feet. The waves lapped at the shore on their left in a steady rhythm and brightly plumed birds darted among the trees and shrubs to her right.

Harriet took a deep breath of scented flowers and fresh sea breezes and wondered if she'd ever felt this happy. Maybe when her parents had been alive, but she had so few memories of that time. A dull throb started at the back of her head and she sent up a prayer that she wouldn't get one of her migraines.

She shook off the thoughts of her parents. This was not the time to think of sad things.

"Thank you for doing this with me, Sol. I need to experience the spa so I'll know how to best showcase it, but I want to be sure I can represent what will appeal to men as well as women."

Solly grinned at her, his brown eyes sparkling. He had the longest, thickest eyelashes she had ever seen on a man. It was really quite unfair. Women paid good money to have eyelashes like Solly's implanted.

"No need to thank me, Harry. I've been looking forward to this ever since you asked. I'm just glad you asked me instead of McDreamy."

"Don't call him that. His name is Alex." She tried to sound stern but couldn't help the grin that stole across her face.

"I stand corrected. *Alex* McDreamy. I admit that I'm curious—just a bit you understand—as to why you asked me and not him."

A blush crept up Harriet's neck. An ex-New York City murder cop, Alex Hayes headed the resort's security department. Secretly she agreed with Solly's assessment—when Alex was close by the man made her pulse pound—and that's exactly why she hadn't asked him to join her at the spa. He was too . . . distracting.

"I didn't ask Alex because I wanted to do this with you," she told Solly firmly. "I'm more comfortable with you than anyone else I know and I trust that you'll tell me the truth without trying to be polite about it."

"What time is our appointment?"

"Ten." Harriet checked her wrist unit. "We'd better get moving or we'll be late. Let's grab a cart."

The resort provided stylish, chrome trimmed, turquoise blue golf carts for the guests and staff to get around the island. The hydrogen-powered carts ran silent and emitted nothing to pollute the island's pristine atmosphere.

Several carts sat outside the stone building that housed Harriet's office. She resisted the urge to stop in and check for messages and slid into the driver's seat of the nearest cart instead. Solly climbed in beside her and they took off.

The spa had been built on a secluded cove on the west side of the island, nestled between the resort proper–which consisted of several office buildings, the two story main hotel, the kitchens, and several dining spots–and the four coves which held the more private guest cottages. Another group of cottages which Harriet had yet to see lay on the island's remote northeast shore.

The amusement park, marina, air pad, and recently opened circus were located on the northwest portion of the island. The resort truly had something for everyone.

"There's the turn-off." Solly pointed to a narrow, almost hidden lane leading off to the left. A four foot tall, pale yellow obelisk with the word "SPA" carved into it marked the narrow lane.

Harriet turned the cart down the side road. Two minutes later they parked at the entrance to the spa.

"Five minutes to spare," she announced, pleased. She hated to be late and usually made sure she arrived at least a few minutes early no matter what the occasion.

They exited the cart and stood looking at the long, window-less pale stone building in front of them. Harriet frowned.

"It doesn't look very luxurious from out here," she said. "I expected the place to be over the top, you know? The rest of the resort meets that 'best in the world' expectation. I would think Mr. Wade would want the spa to be even better."

She turned a slow circle, taking in the pink shell parking pad dotted with palm trees and tall, furry-leaved plants she didn't recognize. Large showy clusters of hanging trumpet shaped flowers in pastel tones of pink, peach, white, and yellow covered the plants.

Harriet took a couple steps closer to one of the flowers and sniffed. The heavy scent made her step hastily back. "What are those flowers? They must be a foot long."

Solly walked over to stand next to Harriet and grinned. "Brugmansia. Also known as Angel's Trumpets. You should smell them at night. They're pollinated by bats so their scent intensifies after sundown. The spa is only open during daylight hours because of them."

"Huh." Harriet headed for the building. "Why did you plant them if they're so offensive?"

Solly held open the heavy, carved wooden door and ushered her inside. "I didn't. They're native to the island and Mr. Wade wanted me to leave them. He decided to limit the spa's hours rather than destroy native fauna."

Harriet's already high opinion of the resort's reclusive owner soared. Someday she hoped to meet the mysterious Mr. Wade so she could thank him for all he'd done for her.

The nondescript outside of the building gave no hint of what waited within. Stepping into the spa was like stepping into another world. Harriet looked about her with wonder. Here was the best in the world spa that she had expected to find.

The lobby wall facing the door was entirely missing. Lush green jungle plants took its place. Small prisms hanging from the roof edge caught the sunlight glinting off the private cove's waters and tossed subtle rainbows into the lobby. Water cascaded quietly down the pale yellow stone wall to Harriet's right, landing in a wide trough filled with white water lilies and brightly colored koi.

The soft tinkle of outside wind chimes blended with the soothing sound of the water wall. Two receptionists dressed in resort-blue skinsuits, one male and one female, stood behind a black granite counter in the center of the lobby waiting to greet them. Genuine smiles were plastered on both of their faces.

Harriet crossed the honey colored wood floor with Solly at her side. "Good morning," she said. She had expected the couple to be droids, as Mr. Wade used droids to fill most of the receptionist positions in the resort, but apparently he had opted to use humans in the spa as these two were definitely human. Human and beautiful.

The woman's hair fell in a silky black curtain down her back to her narrow waist. The hair, combined with her smooth mocha skin and bright blue eyes, dainty nose, and bow-shaped lips proclaimed her mixed ancestry. The male possessed the same mocha coloring and black hair but with mossy green eyes. Their skinsuits revealed every curve and line of their bodies. Both were in incredible physical condition.

Harriet resisted the urge to rub the bump on the bridge of her own rather prominent nose and suppressed an inward sigh. Since she stood five feet eleven inches in her stocking feet, petite women with perfect faces always made her feel like a giant ogress.

It wasn't the receptionist's fault she had great genes Harriet reminded herself while she forced a smile. "I'm Harriet Monroe, the resort PR director. I have a ten o'clock appointment."

The woman tapped a few keys on her PC. "Yes, Miss Monroe, we have you down for the works." Her blue eyes sparkled at Harriet. "You are really going to enjoy this, I promise you. I just need a little information and then the doctor will ask you a few questions before we begin. Have you ever used a spa before?"

Before Harriet could answer, she heard a commotion behind

her and turned. A woman clasping the neck of a thick white robe entered the lobby from an opening next to the water wall. It was difficult to tell the woman's age as her face was covered in cracked, green clay.

The woman stumbled closer to Harriet. Something was off about her face. It took Harriet a moment to realize that it was horribly swollen.

"Mrs. Haggedorn." The female receptionist started around the counter.

"Help. You must . . . help me." The woman reached out a green hand toward Harriet. "Miss . . . take–"

The woman grabbed at Harriet's arm, letting her robe fall open. She wore nothing but a layer of green mud underneath.

"Mrs. Haggedorn, what happened?" The receptionist sounded truly alarmed.

Unfortunately Mrs. Haggedorn was beyond answering. Her knees buckled and she gurgled something Harriet couldn't make out. Her hand slipped from Harriet's arm as Solly caught her and eased her carefully to the floor.

"Do you have a doctor on site?" he asked the hovering receptionist.

"Yes."

"I already called. She'll be here in a few moments." The male receptionist came out from behind the counter.

Solly closed the robe to preserve the woman's modesty. He checked the woman's wrist for her pulse, frowned and tried her neck.

A woman in the familiar white coat that doctors wore everywhere hurried in from the hall opposite the water wall. "What's wrong, Aaron? I was with a client–" she stopped talking as soon as she spied Mrs. Haggedorn on the floor.

Harriet had to admire the doctor's calm efficiency. She wasted no time kneeling next to the unconscious woman and checking her pulse and pupils. She looked at Solly, who knelt on the other side of Mrs. Haggedorn.

"Are you a friend of Mrs. Haggedorn?" she asked.

Solly shook his head. "No. We just got here. She's dead, isn't she?"

CHAPTER TWO

"Dead?" The spa's female receptionist squeaked the word and swayed on her feet.

"What?!" Harriet looked at Solly and the doctor and then down at the unnaturally still, crumpled green body of Mrs. Haggedorn. Bits of the clay body mask had flaked off her skin and dotted the white robe and the floor.

Now that she had a chance to really look at her, the dead woman looked older than Harriet had thought at first. She recalled the glimpse she'd had of Mrs. Haggedorn's naked body. The older woman had possessed good muscle tone and was obviously a woman who took care of her body and treated herself to spas.

And now she was dead.

"Are you sure she's dead?" Harriet whispered. "How can she be dead? And why is her face so bloated?"

Solly stood. "Harry, call Alex."

He turned to the male receptionist who seemed to still have his wits about him. "Aaron?" The receptionist gave a curt nod. "You'd better cancel any other morning appointments."

Harriet fumbled in her knapsack for her link. "Alex," she said, when his face showed on her screen. His face lit up with a smile when he saw who was calling.

"Harriet. What a nice surprise. I was just thinking about you."

Despite the situation, seeing Alex sent a little thrill through Harriet. She couldn't help it–the man had a devastating smile. She hated that she was about to wipe that smile off his face.

"Alex, I'm at the spa with Solly. There's a–" she looked down at Mrs. Haggedorn and felt pity well up in her chest. "A woman just died here. I think you'd better come right away." She heard Alex curse as she cut the connection without waiting for his answer.

Aaron worked his desk link, smoothly notifying guests that the spa was closing for the day due to an emergency and he would reschedule them as soon as possible. Colorful birds twittered in the thick greenery outside the lobby, unaware and uncaring about the drama unfolding inside.

Harriet turned and saw the female receptionist staring down at the body. She appeared to be in shock, her face pale beneath her mocha colored skin.

"I didn't catch your name," Harriet said, touching her arm gently.

The receptionist started. "My name? I-I'm Raylene. I can't believe she's really dead." She twisted her hands until her fingers were white, pulled them apart and shook them out, then twisted her fingers together again.

Raylene's hands were as fine-boned as the rest of her, Harriet noticed. "Has Mrs. Haggedorn been here before?" she asked.

Raylene nodded. "Every day since she came to stay with us last Monday. She usually gets a massage with the hot stone treatment because she says it relaxes her, but today she wanted to try the full seaweed mask." Tears leaked from Raylene's eyes and ran down her cheeks.

"I liked her," she choked out. "She was old, but spunky, you know? And really, really nice. She didn't treat the staff here like she was better than us the way a lot of the guests do. She told me that her husband died about thirty years ago but she got tired of sitting home by herself and started to travel. She likes the resorts best because she likes . . ." Raylene faltered, took a deep breath. "She liked to people watch."

"Come sit down," Harriet urged, seeing the way the receptionist was beginning to shake. She led Raylene back to her chair behind the granite counter and waited for her to sit.

"Does Mrs. Haggedorn have any family that you know of?"

"Family?" Raylene blinked the tears away. "Oh god, her granddaughter will be devastated. Who's going to tell her?"

The loud sound of a combustion engine saved Harriet from having to answer. The noise cut off abruptly and the carved wooden door opened to reveal Alex Hayes, the resort's security director.

Harriet's pulse kicked up again. Alex's broad shoulders filled a good deal of the doorway. He glanced her way as he entered the room but headed straight for the doctor and Solly who had remained standing over Mrs. Haggedorn's body.

Alex held out a hand toward the doctor. "I'm Alex Hayes, head of security. What happened?"

The doctor briefly shook the offered hand. "Doctor Eleanor Clarke. I don't know what happened. Alice Haggedorn was a healthy woman in her seventies. I signed off on her myself when she first came to the spa. Nothing here should have been harmful to her in any way."

Harriet looked over the counter at the lifeless body.

Alice. A normal, healthy widow who liked to travel, and according to Raylene, had spunk and was nice. The advances in medicine over the last century had extended the average human life span to one hundred thirty years. Until this morning Alice had every reason to expect to live another fifty to sixty years. Instead she was dead.

"Are there any other guests in the spa this morning?" Alex

asked.

"Two," answered Aaron. "A married couple–the Humphreys. They requested the special couple's suite located in the opposite end of the spa from Mrs. Haggedorn's treatment room. It has a Japanese style soaking tub and two massage tables. They're due for their massage in . . ." He checked his wrist unit. "Twenty minutes. What should I do about them?"

Alex frowned down at the body. "Cancel the massage but let them be for the time being. Don't let them leave the spa before I have a chance to speak with them."

"Alex? What's wrong?" Harriet came out from behind the counter and joined the group standing near the dead woman. "You don't think–surely you don't suspect a suspicious death."

Don't let this be another murder. "Please tell me her heart just gave out." She turned worried eyes on Alex. He looked grimly back.

Harriet's worry grew.

"Why would a perfectly healthy seventy year old woman die during a spa treatment?" Alex asked her. "Look at her face. Until we can get an autopsy done I have to rule this a suspicious death."

He turned to Aaron. "Round up everyone working here this morning please. And set me up in a private space where I can interview them."

"Oh, no. Not again." Harriet collapsed on the short wall edging the koi pool and put her head in her hands. If Mrs. Haggedorn had been murdered then she had another public relations nightmare on her hands.

The resort had only recently recovered from its first murder, partly because of the new Murder Mystery Nights held in the hotel's second largest restaurant, and partly because people tended to be macabre and liked to visit crime scenes. Jack the Ripper tours still drew crowds centuries after the serial killer stopped preying on London prostitutes.

The spa was one of the big draws for the exclusive resort.

Harriet wasn't sure she could find a way to overcome the bad publicity if it turned out that Mrs. Haggedorn had really been murdered here.

She felt a body sit next to her and knew it was Solly. He gently drew her hands away from her face.

"Buck up, kid," he drawled. "It's only the second body we've found since you've been here. Things could be worse."

Harriet scowled at her friend. "How? How could they be worse, Sol? People will be afraid to book a visit with us because they'll be afraid of being murdered while they're here. Two bodies in what—less than six weeks time? It's–it's . . . diabolical. That's what it is. The pundits are going to change our name from Island Resort to Murder Resort. What am I going to do?"

"I'll tell you what you're not going to do," rumbled a deep voice from her other side.

Harriet swiveled and looked into Alex's deep blue eyes. His crooked nose and the scar over his right eyebrow should have made him look like a street thug. Instead they added character to the unmistakably confident masculinity that oozed from his every pore. Solly rated Alex a "hubba-hubba" on their personal yardstick of sexiness. Harriet had to agree. She might even add another hubba.

Solly had been encouraging her to act on her attraction to Alex, but Harriet had been taking it slow. She'd made a terrible mistake with a man once before and wanted to be sure before she put her heart in that vulnerable position again.

Looking at Alex now, she reluctantly admitted that it might already be too late for her heart. Somehow he had snuck beneath her defenses and made himself at home.

"What aren't I going to do?" she asked him. She could feel the heat Alex's body gave off even in the cool interior of the spa's lobby and wished he'd wrap his arms around her. She could use a little comforting.

She shook off the thought and straightened her shoulders.

She was a professional, she reminded herself. It was time to act like one.

"You aren't going to panic," Alex said, watching Harriet closely. Finding a dead body so soon after the last one would shake anyone. When he saw her straighten her shoulders he knew she'd be okay.

"Alice Haggedorn's death is not your fault. You just happened to be here when she died."

"She nearly died in my arms." Harriet shuddered. "The poor woman. I wonder what happened."

Alex stood. "I intend to find out. I'm afraid I'll need you both to stay here until I interview you formally. I've called Fox to give me a hand. He should be here any minute." He gave Harriet's shoulder a gentle squeeze and walked back to where Mrs. Haggedorn still lay. Someone had covered the body with a white sheet.

The spa door opened. Harriet turned her head, expecting to see Tarbell Fox, Alex's new second in command, but a young woman walked in instead.

"The spa is closed," Alex called out to her.

The woman stopped and furrowed her brow. "Closed? It can't be. I'm supposed to meet my grandmother here. Alice Haggedorn? I'm her granddaughter, Sequoia Haggedorn?"

Sequoia stepped forward and held out her hand toward Alex. Harriet noticed that she wore brightly jeweled rings on every finger of both hands. In fact "bright" was a good word for Sequoia.

Her short hair, cut into a cap that closely fit her skull and framed a mischievous looking face, was bright red. Her eyes shone more gold than brown over sharp cheekbones, a wide, full mouth, and a pointed chin.

Harriet estimated her slender body stood somewhere near five feet six. Her age was harder to guess. Mid-twenties, maybe thirty?

The color didn't stop with the rings and hair. Sequoia wore

silky harem pants in a swirling pattern of lime green and orange that sat low on rounded hips. She'd paired the pants with a neon fuchsia pink bandeau top that made Harriet's eyes want to spin in her head. The midriff baring outfit revealed a gleaming ruby-colored stone in Sequoia's tanned navel.

"There's a gal who likes attention," Solly murmured in Harriet's ear.

"I'm sorry to meet you under such unpleasant circumstances," Alex said, taking Sequoia's hand briefly in his own and releasing it.

"Unpleasant? Whatever do you mean?" She gave Alex's arm a playful slap. "This place is wonderful."

Alex nodded his head toward the sheet covered body.

"I regret to inform you that your grandmother has died."

Sequoia put a hand to her throat. "Died?" She shook her head. "No. You must be mistaken. Gamma is in excellent condition."

"I'd like you to make a positive identification of the deceased for me please, Miss Haggedorn. That way we'll both know there's no mistake."

"Of course it's a mistake," Sequoia said crossly. "Gamma isn't dead."

She stalked over to the body and pulled off the sheet. "Gamma? Oh my god, it's Gamma. What happened to her face?"

Alex had followed her over to the body. Sequoia turned and threw herself at his chest, sobbing. "My Gamma is dead," she wailed.

Alex looked over the sobbing woman's head at Solly and Harriet.

"Think he wants us to help?" Solly asked softly.

The spa door opened again, this time to admit Tarbell Fox's burly frame. Harriet saw him hesitate a moment when he caught sight of the sobbing woman in Alex's arms, then sigh and walk forward.

"Let them handle it," Harriet answered. "They're the pros."

CHAPTER THREE

Solly and Harriet remained seated on the edge of the koi fountain while the spa staff was interviewed. The water flowed quietly down the wall behind them before pooling softly into the fish pond.

Aaron brought them fruit drinks and then sat at his station while he waited his turn as Raylene sobbed quietly beside him.

Fox appeared and called the receptionists and the trio disappeared down the wing opposite the hall from which Alice Haggedorn had appeared an hour earlier.

Fifteen minutes later Harriet watched Aaron lead Raylene out the door with his arm about her shoulders. Raylene had her face buried in the handsome receptionist's side.

Two well-toned women and a man, all three dressed in outfits similar to Korean doboks—loose tops and pants worn for martial arts practice—left next, followed by a subdued looking middle-aged couple ten minutes later.

"Masseur, masseuses, and the Humphreys, I gather," Solly said, gently brushing the petals of a waterlily. "Ever notice how soft flower petals are? We should be next."

Harriet was used to the way Solly's mind jumped around. She

understood that he meant next for interviews. "Are you sorry you came with me today? This isn't quite how I imagined our spa treat."

Solly stopped playing with the flower. "No. I'm glad I came. Mrs. Haggedorn looked a little frightening coming into the lobby the way she did, didn't she? Poor old gal. Her face all blown up like a balloon, all green and stumbling. She looked like some graphic novel monster. Although I guess if she was having a heart attack or a seizure of some kind you would expect her to be stumbling, wouldn't you? And I'm just rambling."

He sighed and clasped Harriet's nearest hand. "I feel bad that this is happening to you again. You do realize that the staff is going to start calling you 'Murder Monroe.' Or 'Homicide Harry.' He snapped his fingers. "No, wait, I've got it–instead of PR director they'll be calling you the 'Director of Death'."

A laugh escaped Harriet's lips before she could stop it. Leave it to Solly to find the humor in a lousy situation. When they'd been young, homeless runaways back in Maine, Solly had always found something to make her smile about. It was one of the many reasons he was her closest friend and she loved him as dearly as she would a brother.

Dr. Clarke looked up from the bench she'd taken near the open wall and glared at Harriet, making her feel guilty about laughing when a dead woman's body lay not twenty feet away.

"Dr. Clarke." Fox appeared and beckoned to the doctor. "Come with me please." They disappeared from sight.

"I'm ready for you." Alex appeared at their side and led them into the wing next to the water wall.

Harriet found herself in a wide corridor closed in on one side by a solid stone wall and on the other by a muraled wall broken up by a series of lattice-framed doors filled with translucent paper. "Do the doors lead to treatment rooms?" she asked.

"Yes. Aaron tells me the doors are Japanese and called shōji." Alex stopped next to the nearest shōji and slid it open to reveal a room that opened onto the jungled cove the same way the lobby did.

"All of the treatment rooms have only three walls, but because there is no outside walkway they're all very private." He closed the door and continued down the hall with Solly and Harriet following.

This really wasn't how she had pictured her morning going, mused Harriet. She was supposed to be lying on one of those treatment tables getting a full body massage. She stifled a sigh, but Solly must have heard her because he squeezed her fingers briefly.

Alex stopped in front of an open shōji. "This is the room where Alice Haggedorn received her treatment. I've dusted for prints and searched it already. I'd like you both to take a look and give me your thoughts." He stepped to the side of the doorway without entering the room.

The first thing Harriet noticed when she entered was the size. She had expected the treatment rooms to be narrow in order to maximize the space and to fit as many as possible into the building, but the room felt spacious. As with everything else on the resort Mr. Wade had gone for quality over quantity.

The second thing she noticed was the fine, black fingerprint powder over most of the surfaces.

The two side walls were covered in a pale, reed-textured wall covering that helped tie the room to the jungle just outside. Soft music emitted from hidden speakers. An unseen wind chime with a deep, pleasing tone sounded softly as a breeze rustled through the palm fronds.

A thigh high massage table occupied the center of the room. Draped in a white sheet that was topped with a translucent plastic sheet, it still held smears of dried green clay.

"The plastic sheet protects the resort linens from the clay," Alex said as he watched them from the door. "Apparently the used ones get hosed off and are reused several times before getting tossed into the trash. According to the masseuse who treated Mrs. Haggedorn today, they also wrap the guest in the plastic to hold in body heat."

Harriet didn't touch the sheet. She wandered to the left side wall where a pale gray granite counter held a collection of scented massage oils and two pieces of equipment. Recognizing the lemony, herbaceous smell of lemongrass she located the diffuser in the center of the counter and breathed in the pleasing scent.

She lifted the cover from one of the larger pieces of equipment and found the remainder of the slowly bubbling clay mask that had been used on Alice Haggedorn. The clay was a pretty pale mossy green with flecks of deeper green throughout. An herb, perhaps?

She replaced the cover. "This is still on. Should I turn it off?"

"Not yet. The other heating unit is used for the hot stone treatment."

Harriet slid back the lid of the square stone heater and looked inside. Smooth disc-shaped rocks ranging in color from black to palest gray filled the heater. She felt one. They were hot. Had Mrs. Haggedorn intended to have a hot stone treatment in addition to her clay body mask?

Alex might have been reading her mind. "According to Raylene the hot stone treatment was Alice Haggedorn's preferred treatment. She was trying something new today at the urging of her granddaughter."

Something in Alex's voice made Harriet turn her head and look at him. "The granddaughter seemed honestly upset about her grandmother's death," she said carefully.

"Yes. She did." Alex said no more and Harriet continued her exploration of the room.

"What's to keep someone from approaching the treatment rooms from the jungle side?" she asked as she walked to the floor's outside edge. She saw that the room hung a good ten feet beyond a precipitous drop off. That was why the spa felt as if it was built in the treetops, she realized–the back edge of the building must have been at least thirty feet or more above the ground.

"Isn't Mr. Wade afraid that a guest might fall off the edge?" she asked, frowning.

"The treatment rooms in the other wing have waist high plexiglass walls for anyone worried about falling, or anyone too young to trust."

Harriet scowled down at the ground. She didn't have a death wish but she didn't feel quite comfortable standing on the edge either. She felt a temptation to fling herself into the trees and quickly turned away, making a mental note to contact Mr. Wade and recommend he install the plexiglass partial walls in all of the treatment rooms before someone fell and sued the resort.

Solly was standing at the floor's outer edge next to a side wall. The wall extended a good four feet beyond the floor's edge. "I don't think anyone could climb around this wall if you're thinking someone came in here and did Alice Haggedorn in," he said, turning to look at Alex. "Even with an open wall these rooms are completely private and accessible only from the hall."

"Dr. Clarke insists that Alice was a healthy seventy year old woman who took excellent care of herself and should have lived at least another half century. She was up to date on her cancer vaccine, never smoked, drank only lightly and ate healthy foods." He scowled at them both. "She could have been a role model for how to live well. I don't like it."

"So you're leaning toward murder," Solly said, leaving the open wall and joining Alex. "How was it done?"

Alex's scowl deepened. "I don't know–yet. But I can think of a few possibles. What if someone climbed one of those trees and nailed her with a poison dart?

Solly looked interested. "That would work. Did you find a dart?"

"No. I've searched this room and the hall."

"Too bad. That would have told you it was definitely murder. What else have you thought of?"

Alex nodded toward the end of the wall next to Solly. "With the right equipment someone could easily scale that wall from the next room and surprise the victim."

Solly took a closer look at the wall, then walked across the room to inspect the wall opposite. "I don't see any scratches or gouges to indicate that someone did that. These walls are nearly brand new and still pristine."

He turned back to Alex, fully caught up now. "What else do you have?"

"My favorite theory, and one I'm not ready to share until after the autopsy. I don't even know if it was murder, or if Dr. Clarke missed something when she initially checked Mrs. Haggedorn out. I'll know in a day or two. Dr. Clarke just left for the mainland with the body. She'll perform the autopsy at the nearest facility with a full lab."

"Does the spa have to remain closed until you get results?" Harriet asked. She was beginning to feel that troubleshooting made up most of her job duties. If problems continued to pile up for the resort she was going to become the century's best spin doctor. "There will be a lot of disappointed guests if they can't use the spa. It's a big draw for the resort."

Alex shook his head. "Not to worry. We'll close this room but keep the rest of the spa operating." He smiled briefly at her visible relief. "I know your job hasn't been easy. Having to deal with one murder right after your arrival was bad enough. We'll keep the investigation into Alice Haggedorn's death as low-key as possible."

"Great. I appreciate it."

Alex sealed the treatment room when they left.

Unfortunately his plan to keep any investigation quiet blew up in his face as soon as he returned to his office.

CHAPTER FOUR

Fifteen minutes after parting from Harry and Solly Alex approached the two story office building that housed the security office and his apartment overhead. Like the other resort offices, it was built of thick, pale stone walls and sported a thatched roof.

Few people knew that the thatch camouflaged sturdy cement roofs. Mr. Wade had designed his resort to withstand the category four and five hurricanes that liked to sweep the islands on occasion, often leaving utter destruction in their wake. The thatch would blow away and do no harm, while the buildings safely protected anyone inside riding out the storm.

Alex entered the building and stepped into chaos. The tasteful and usually quiet security lobby held at least two dozen resort guests. They filled the blue and green upholstered chairs that lined the wall on either side of the heavy wooden door and crowded around the waist high counter that faced the door.

One of his security droids–they were all named Mary and looked exactly alike with short black hair and pug noses–calmly faced the clamoring guests. The frown lines etched between Mary's dark eyebrows were a permanent feature of her face, the designer's way of giving the droid a serious demeanor, so it was difficult for Alex to tell how she was handling the crowd.

He walked across the gleaming wood floor toward the counter, gently muscling aside the knots of complaining guests without being too rude. He slid behind the counter and stood beside Mary.

"What's the problem here?" he asked her quietly.

"These people want to know what we're doing about the unsafe conditions on the island. They heard about the death at the spa."

Alex's stomach clenched. So much for keeping Alice Haggedorn's death quiet. He wondered if Harriet's phone was already ringing off the hook with calls from the other department heads. Raising his hands like a pope giving benediction to the masses he called for silence.

"Excuse me, people." It took several minutes for everyone to stop talking and look at him. Alex waited patiently. He had no intention of trying to talk over everyone. He'd learned from his time on the force that speaking with quiet authority commanded more attention than shouting. When he was sure every last guest was looking at him and listening he continued.

"Apparently some of you have heard about the passing of one of our guests. While we do not know any details at this time, I can assure you that her death was not caused by any negligence on the part of the resort."

"That's not what we heard," called a man from one of the chairs.

Alex sized up the speaker. Tanned, expensive watch and haircut, wearing the latest in resort fashion. An executive, used to pushing his weight around the boardroom and getting his way. "Just what have you heard, Mr.–?"

"Eames. Jeffrey Eames. President and CEO of Collider Investments."

Alex allowed himself an inward smirk. Nailed it.

"The dead woman's granddaughter told *me* that her grandmother died while having a spa treatment. You're supposed to check the guests out before they have a treatment. The woman's death is obviously the fault of the spa doctor."

"Only part of what you said is true, Mr. Eames. I can assure you that Alice Haggedorn was thoroughly checked out before her treatment and was found to be in remarkably good health. We do not yet know what killed her and it is premature and foolish of you to jump to conclusions when the facts are not all in."

The tips of Jeffrey Eames' ears reddened.

Alex sighed. Making enemies of the guests was not in his best interest.

"We don't believe you."

Alex sought out the speaker. A handsome man around his own age, with spiky, blonde-tipped blue hair and several silver hoops dangling from his left ear stepped out from behind a small knot of people and crossed his arms over his well-formed chest. His arms bulged with pumped up muscle. He wore a cynical smirk on his tanned face and a gleam in his electric blue eyes.

Alex took in the dyed hair, colored contact lenses, and jewelry. Body builder narcissist. Liked to be the center of attention. The man had troublemaker written all over him. Alex had often dealt with the same type when he worked the streets of New York City. This was a man who believed he was smarter than everyone else and wanted everyone to know it.

"Your name?" Alex asked.

"Terence Leighton. Miss Haggedorn told me what happened. You're lying to us."

A murmur swept through the security office lobby.

Alex made a huge effort to hold onto his temper.

"Mr. Leighton, how can I be lying to you when I don't yet know enough about what happened to Mrs. Haggedorn to know what I should be lying about? Give us a chance to do our job. If we find any hint of negligence on the part of the spa's staff the guests will be notified and the spa immediately closed until we can rectify the problem."

Terence Leighton's smirk widened. "Yeah, right. Like we can trust you to tell us the truth. You're one of Mr. Wade's stooges. You'll do whatever he tells you to do because he signs your paycheck. Wade is the richest man in the world, right? He owns you and everyone else who works for him."

He looked around at the other guests. "No point staying here. We aren't going to get the truth from *Security Director* Hayes."

There was grumbling and ugly looks cast Alex's way as the guests filed out of the office after Terence Leighton.

"That man is a real prick."

Alex looked at his assistant with surprise. "Fox. I didn't see you come in."

"I beat you back from the spa. I was in the office running background checks on the spa staff when the mob turned up led by the asshole in the blue hair. They were waiting for you so I stayed in the background. Thought it might be wiser unless you needed backup. You know how mobs can get ugly if they think they're being threatened."

"Yeah." Alex looked thoughtfully at the door. "I want you to add Jeffrey Eames to your background checks. I'll take Terence Leighton and the Haggedorns."

Under normal circumstances, Alex would have run background checks on every resort employee during the hiring process, but he'd been brought in late and most of the staff had already been hired by the time he had started the job.

"Did you learn anything interesting about the spa staff?" he asked Fox. He stepped over to the hot and cold drinks center next to the counter and poured himself a glass of the fresh squeezed lemonade that the kitchen stocked for him. Downing the tart-sweet citrusy drink he set the glass in the dirty dish tray to be picked up at the end of the day and waited for Fox's report.

Tarbell Fox had recently come onto Alex's radar while Alex

had been hunting a murderer on the island. An ex-cop who'd been wrongfully terminated by a corrupt superior and unable to work as a police officer again, Fox had taken a job as a bellhop at the resort. Luckily for Alex he'd been happy to transfer to the resort's security department and quickly stepped into the role of Alex's right-hand man.

Fox pulled out his pocket PC and found his notes.

"Aaron Woo, aged twenty three, receptionist at the spa since opening. Family is from Atlanta, Georgia, three younger sisters, parents typical middle working class, no blots on record for any of them. Good student, no significant others listed.

"Raylene Brown, aged twenty one, only child. Mother is a professor of criminology at Michigan State University in East Lansing, Michigan."

Alex's eyebrows rose.

"Yup. That caught my attention too. Father is a CPA. Owns his own accounting firm. Raylene did accelerated classes and graduated two years early with a degree in accounting, then took a year to work at the resort before she joins her father's firm."

"Okay. Probably nothing there. Go on."

Fox checked his notes again. "Dr. Eleanor Clarke specializes in general medicine. Isn't that an oxymoron?"

"What do you mean?"

"How can someone specialize in something general?"

"General medicine just means the doctor doesn't specialize in blood or brain diseases or something focused like that. Dr. Clarke is what they used to refer to as a GP–the family doctor, or a general practitioner. Continue, please."

"Right. She's clean. Divorced, two adult children, one of each. No debt, lives simply, seems devoted to her work." He shrugged. "I didn't pick up on any hinky vibe when I interviewed her. She's very serious and focused on her work. Told me she took this job to get away from cities for a while, wanted to commune with nature or something."

"Okay. Dr. Clarke goes to the bottom of our list along with Raylene Brown and Aaron Woo. Add Dr. Clarke's children to your background checks just in case. Maybe one of them hates Mommy and is trying to sabotage her position at the resort."

Fox leaned against the counter and crossed his legs. "So you're thinking Alice Haggedorn's death is a homicide."

Alex took a deep breath, blew it out. "It has that feel–I'm not sure why, but it felt like a homicide as soon as I saw the body. Some just hit that way, you know?"

Fox agreed and returned to his notes. "All right. We have three masseuses. Or I should say we have two masseuses and one masseur who were working while Haggedorn was there. Those terms are French by the way. Leave it to the French to coin a term for rubbing someone else's body."

Alex rolled his hand, telling his assistant to stay on topic.

"Right. Two more masseuses were scheduled to work later in the day so that makes five total employed by the spa."

Alex thought about that for a minute. Five massage therapists and twelve treatment rooms. Even fully booked it was a schedule they could easily handle.

"Start with the three who were working this morning."

Fox read off the information but nothing struck Alex as useful. "Put them on the bottom of the list and run Eames next. I'll run the Haggedorn females and Terence Leighton as soon as I get back."

"Do you need me to come with you?"

"Nope. I just want to make sure that mob didn't head over to Harriet's office. I'll call if I need you."

CHAPTER FIVE

Harriet hurried back to Mermaid Cottage to change into an office appropriate outfit. She had a feeling that Cassandra Montgomery, their resort manager, would soon be swamped with questions. It didn't matter that Alex had told everyone to keep quiet about Alice Haggedorn's death–a dead body, especially one slathered in green clay, was too juicy a topic for gossip. People would talk.

Solly headed off for his beloved greenhouses on foot, leaving Harriet the use of the golf cart to get to her own office. She pulled on her sandals and slid a pair of heels that matched her pale sage silk suit into her knapsack, locked the cottage after her, and made it to her office in ten minutes. She switched to her heels and left the golf cart parked for anyone who needed it.

Pulling open the heavy wooden door with its stained glass insert, Harriet let herself into the office building's spacious lobby. The handsome droid who manned the lobby desk smiled at her.

"I did not expect to see you in the office today, Miss Monroe," he said, in the clipped British accent that Harriet loved. Jeeves wore his customary cream colored linen suit with a resort blue shirt. A neatly folded blue handkerchief peeked from his breast pocket.

"Change of plans, Jeeves. And please call me Harry. I thought I'd put a few hours in after all."

"In that case, I should tell you that Ms. Montgomery was looking for you a short while ago. I told her you were taking a spa treatment. She indicated that she would wait until tomorrow to contact you."

"Thank you, Jeeves. I'll go find Cassie and see what she needs." Jeeves released the lock on the door that protected the hallway leading to several of the offices and Harriet slid through it with another thank you. While some considered it foolish to waste good manners on a droid, they were so lifelike that Harriet felt they deserved the same courtesy she gave to others.

In his usual thorough fashion, Douglas Wade had extended his creation of the high-end resort to include the office hallway even though it was a utilitarian space not seen by the general public.

Harriet's heels clicked on the wide floor's large creamy white tiles as she hurried toward Cassie's office. Frond-bladed fans twirled lazily over her head. Frescoes of the island painted by a renowned native artist covered the entire righthand wall.

The left wall sported tall, narrow windows that let in light but didn't open for security reasons. There wasn't much to see—the windows looked out on the crushed shell road and the kitchen building opposite, but the views from the individual offices more than made up for the lack of view in the hallway.

Harriet knocked on Cassie's door, cleverly camouflaged in a depiction of Black Bart's Cove with its historic, partially sunken schooner. She heard a harried "Come in!" and let herself into her friend's office.

Like Harriet's office space, Cassie's was spacious and looked out over the beach and water. A family with four children were riding skim boards on the shallow waves at the sand's edge.

Harriet watched the youngest girl run and toss her board, then chase after it when her leap missed. She'd have to try skim boarding herself one day, she mused. It looked like fun.

"Harry! Thank goodness you're here. Jeeves said you were having a spa treatment so I didn't call. Boy, am I glad to see you!" Cassie heaved her large body from her desk chair and headed for her chiller. Her royal purple caftan–a clothing style she typically wore–swirled around her ample curves.

"Lemonade?" she asked over her shoulder.

"I'd love some. I had to change my clothes or I would have been here sooner." Harriet lowered herself onto one of the brightly cushioned chairs set around a glass table and accepted the glass of lemonade.

Where the style of Harriet's office was subdued, Cassie's office reflected her love for bright colors. The furniture, rugs, and artwork depicting island life were all done in strong, tropical hues. Jan Rhymes, the interior designer hired by Douglas Wade for the resort, had captured Cassidy's and Harriet's individual personalities and reflected them perfectly in their work spaces.

Cassie poured herself a fruit spritzer, sat, and leaned forward. "So, tell me all and then help me figure out how to handle this," she said.

"How much do you know? It's supposed to be hush-hush."

Cassie waved Harriet's words away. "Oh please. Forget hush-hush. The death of Alice Haggedorn is all over the resort. Sequoia Haggedorn went straight from the spa to the large dining room—acting suitably tragic I might add–and told everyone that her grandmother had been killed at the spa. What happened? You were there, weren't you?"

Harriet frowned. "Yes. I actually saw her die." She didn't say that the poor woman had practically died in her arms.

Cassie's eyes widened. "Oh. Poor Harriet. Two dead bodies in less than two month's time." She patted Harriet's hand in sympathy. "Why did she die?"

"We don't know. Dr. Clarke took the bod–took Mrs. Haggedorn to a lab on the mainland and is doing an autopsy to get some answers. The thing is, Cass, she shouldn't have died. She was only seventy and very healthy."

Cassie sat back in her seat and sipped her drink thoughtfully. "Has Alex said anything to you?"

"He's suspicious. He let Solly and me check out the room where she was getting her treatment. Have you seen the spa rooms? No one could have gotten to her unless they went through the door."

"I've not only seen them, I have a standing weekly appointment. Massage and hot stones. It keeps me sane. You should try it by the way. Your job is as stressful as mine, especially now." She gave Harriet a knowing look which Harriet ignored.

"Fine. Don't take my advice. Getting back to Alice Haggedorn, you're right, the only way into those rooms is through the doors."

Cassie's desk link had buzzed several times while they talked. It buzzed again, sounding more insistent to Harriet's ears if that was possible.

"Do you want to get that?" she asked.

Cassie shook her head. "Not yet. I'm sure it's the reservations office, wondering what to tell people when they start to call. What should I tell them?"

Harriet grimaced. "Tell them the truth, I guess. We don't yet know what happened to Mrs. Haggedorn and you'll contact them as soon as you have more information. There really isn't anything else you can say."

Cassie heaved a sigh as the link buzzed again. "Guess I'd better talk to them. Thanks for stopping by."

Harriet stood and hugged her friend. "I'll let you know as soon as I learn anything. Even if it turns out to be a natural death maybe we should make it into a murder and add it to our Murder Mystery Dinner repertoire." She waggled her eyebrows, making Cassie laugh.

"Get out of here. Go PR for us so we don't lose business. I'd hate to get a call from Mr. Wade demanding to know why revenue has dropped."

Harriet hurried back down the hallway to her own office. Her office door was camouflaged at the base of a green mountain, the security panel hidden in a slim waterfall. Placing her hand on the palm reader, she keyed in her personal code once it flashed. The mountain section slid silently open and Harriet entered her office, immediately kicking off her heels.

She walked barefoot over to the glass doors opposite and opened them, letting in a soft warm breeze that carried the scent of the sea and exotic blossoms. She took a few moments to enjoy the beauty outside her office, then turned to the wall of shelves and picked up the antique, cherry framed hologram of her parents.

"Hi, Mom. Hi, Dad." Her mother, dressed in a long, pale green robe, smiled out at her. Her father, tall and handsome with Harriet's silver-blue eyes and strong chin, stood with his arms wrapped around her mother. They looked happy, their love forever frozen in time. Would they have looked that happy if they had lived?

"I found another body today. Well, I didn't really find her. It was more that she found me. Solly says my co-workers are going to start calling me 'Murder Monroe'. Pretty funny, huh?"

Harriet's throat suddenly clogged with unshed tears. She set the holo back on the shelf. "Miss you guys," she whispered. A familiar dull ache in the back of her head started and she turned away to get a bottled water, but a knock sounded on the door before she could cross the room.

She veered toward the door and hit the open switch. Alex filled the doorway, his hands in the pockets of his khakis, a concerned expression on his face. Harriet felt ridiculously pleased to see him.

"Jeeves sent me back," he explained as he entered the office. "Is everything all right here?"

"Of course, why wouldn't it be?" Harriet gave Alex a puzzled look, pulled a bottled water from her chiller, and held it out to him.

He took it and sank into one of her cushioned chairs, stacked his heels on the low bamboo coffee table, and looked around Harriet's office. Jan Rhymes had opted for muted colors for Harriet's space—soft turquoise rugs, large rattan arm chairs with pale peach cushions, light bamboo flooring. It was warm, comfortable, and soothing. Much like Harriet.

"Why were you concerned, Alex?" Harriet asked again as she took a seat opposite.

"There was a welcoming committee at the security office when I got back. You might even call it a small mob. Apparently Sequoia Haggedorn didn't understand when I told her not to mention her grandmother's death until we know exactly what happened. She must have blabbed it all over the island."

Harriet grimaced. "Starting with the large hotel restaurant, I'm afraid. Between the help and the other guests it probably didn't take long to get around."

"I thought you and Cass might be under siege so I came over to see if you needed any help. There were two men in my mob who were particularly unpleasant."

Harriet waved her water bottle, indicating the empty office. "As you can see, all is well, although Cassie's link is buzzing non stop. I imagine we'll have the usual cancellations followed by the ghouls who want to be close to a death scene."

They sat drinking their water in a companionable silence for several minutes before Alex stood and wandered over to the open French doors. "It's hard to believe we could have two murders in such a short time frame in such a beautiful place."

Harriet joined him. The family of skim-boarders have moved

far down the beach. "You believe Mrs. Haggedorn was murdered, then?"

Alex turned his head to look at her. He didn't have to look down far as Harriet stood only four inches shorter than his own six foot three. He wouldn't have to bend far to kiss her either, he thought.

She looked steadily back at him with those strangely arresting silver blue eyes and he felt the familiar desire for her that had plagued him since they'd met less than two months ago.

"Alex? You think she was murdered?"

Alex forced himself away from the pleasant dream of seducing Harriet Monroe and focused on the problem at hand.

"It's the only thing that makes sense," he said. "Unless she had some hidden health issue or allergy that nobody was aware of, there was absolutely no reason for her to die this morning."

"Allergy?" Harriet recalled the woman's bloated face and brightened. An allergic reaction was an accident, something out of the resort's control. "That would explain the swollen face."

"Yes. The problem is that nothing in any of the spa products would trigger an allergic reaction. The product line was thoroughly tested and is closely monitored for consistent quality."

"Oh." Harriet's brief optimism deflated. "So you're back to a suspicious death."

"Yep." Alex stepped away from the open door. "Seeing as you're all right I'd better get back to my office and see what I can dig up on Alice Haggedorn and her granddaughter."

He started toward the hall door but veered toward the shelves when he noticed the hologram. Picking it up, he looked from it to Harriet. "These must be your folks. You have your father's eyes and stubborn chin and your mother's nose and beautiful honey colored hair."

Harriet resisted the urge to take the holo from Alex's hands. "I lost them in an accident when I was quite young. That's all I have of them. My aunt gave it to me."

That was a lie, but Alex didn't need to know that Harriet had found the holo tucked away in an otherwise empty cardboard box in her aunt's attic. She had taken it with her when she ran away which meant that technically she had stolen it, but surely her aunt would have given it to her one day.

Alex's eyes were steady on her as he carefully set the holo back on its shelf. "What kind of accident?"

"I don't know. My aunt never said. I assumed it was a car or maybe a tram crash. She only said they died instantaneously and then she refused to talk about it again."

The familiar dull throb started beating in Harriet's skull again. Damn migraines. She'd suffered from them for as long as she could remember, although they varied a great deal in intensity and never lasted long.

Alex gave her a strange look. "I'll let myself out. Call my office if either Terence Leighton or Jeffrey Eames show up here. They're trouble."

Harriet waved him off as she dug in her knapsack for the headache pills she always carried with her.

Alex stood outside Harriet's office and frowned at the closed door. His cop radar fairly quivered. Why had Harriet lied about her parents' death? Could it be that she honestly didn't know the truth behind how they had died?

Impossible. He knew from his research that Harriet had been present when her parents had died.

He didn't like being lied to. Somehow he had to find a way to get to the bottom of why Harriet had lied to him. It was possible that she felt ashamed of her parents. But then why keep their hologram in her office? He made a note to himself to contact Harriet Monroe's aunt and have a talk with her.

That would have to wait however. Right now he needed to get to the bottom of a more recent unexpected and unexplained death.

CHAPTER SIX

Harriet settled down to work on her latest PR campaign for the resort after Alex left. Until they knew why Alice Haggedorn had died there was nothing she could do to help the resort public relations-wise so she might as well focus on her current project.

Creating ad campaigns for the Island Resort, forging relationships with the media and various international governments, and looking for opportunities and ways that businesses could utilize the resort made Harriet's job interesting as well as satisfying.

She loved her job. Loved living on the island. She'd only been there six weeks but she already knew that she'd made the right choice trading the cold snowy winters of Portland, Maine for the tropical island paradise that she now called home.

Deeply immersed in her outline for a new pet project–getting businesses to pay for a program that would bring groups of disadvantaged children to the island for a week at a time–she didn't hear her link buzz. Someone pounded on her door a minute later and called her name.

"Harry! Open up!"

Harriet saved and closed her work and hurried to the door.

"I'm coming. Coming, coming." She hit the release and found Payson Douglas standing in the hallway.

"Payson?" Harriet gave the white-haired, elegant gentleman in her doorway a puzzled frown. "Did we have a date?"

"Harry, you're all right? When you didn't answer your link I became worried."

Payson Douglas was a close friend of the resort's owner and occupied a cottage on Kidd's Cove. Judging from the changes he had made to the cottage, Harriet assumed that it was not included with the other rental cottages and that it had become Payson's permanent home. The older man had befriended her shortly after her arrival and they had a standing Thursday lunch date.

"No, no date," he answered, shaking his head. "I just spoke with Alex and learned about Mrs. Haggedorn. He expressed concern about you and Cassandra so I thought I'd stop by and see if you needed anything from Mr. Wade, but you didn't answer your link even though Jeeves assured me you were in your office."

"Oh." Harriet flushed. She often became so wrapped up in her work that the outside world ceased to exist. "I'm so sorry I worried you. I have a new idea that I was working on and I must have gotten caught up. Won't you come in?"

"I will. But only long enough to assure me that you are truly all right after your experience this morning."

They settled in Harriet's chairs after Payson declined her offer of lemonade. She waited for his intelligent pale blue eyes to look over the office and then her before smiling at him.

"Satisfied?" she asked with a warm smile. "I'm fine. I admit that I was a little shaky earlier, but I'm truly fine now, I promise."

She found Payson's concern for her endearing. She wasn't sure why the older man had taken an interest in her–it was nothing sexual, he acted more like a favorite uncle–but she felt grateful for his interest. She had no one other than Solly and she cherished the friendships she was beginning to forge in her new life on the island.

"You are very resilient, my dear." Payson crossed his long slim legs at the ankles and steepled his fingers. Harriet wondered if Payson played piano–he had the hands for it–but she refrained from asking.

"So, tell me about this morning."

Harriet told him the story, leaving nothing out. Payson had a sharp mind and she was curious to hear his take on Alice Haggedorn's death. He listened without interrupting and sat silent for several minutes afterward.

"You met the granddaughter?" he asked finally.

"Yes. She came to pick up her grandmother." Harriet hesitated.

Payson raised his eyebrows. "And?" he prompted.

"I don't know that there is an 'and'. Sequoia Haggedorn is . . . flamboyant, I guess you could say." She grimaced. "And that sounds so prissy. I believe that she was honestly upset about her grandmother's death, but Alex asked her to keep quiet about it until we know why she died and the story was all over the resort twenty minutes later."

Harriet shrugged. "It just feels wrong, but I guess people handle grief in different ways. Sequoia Haggedorn wears hers in public. I have no right to be judgmental."

Payson stood. "You do have a right to listen to your gut instincts, however. Obviously something feels off to you concerning the young Miss Haggedorn." He headed to the door with Harriet following.

"I'll let you get back to your work, dear. Thank you for putting an old man's mind to rest." He turned back toward her when he reached the door. "By the way, what's this new idea you're working on?"

Harriet blushed. "Oh, it's a pet project I've had in the back of my mind since I arrived. I want to bring groups of disadvantaged children to the resort for a week or two at a time." She saw Payson's eyebrows go up and hastened to explain her plan.

"I'm hoping to get different corporate sponsors to cover the costs. I think I can convince them that it will be good advertisement for their companies. If the program is successful then they'll be fighting for the chance to support it. Ooh."

She hurried to her desk and jotted down a note. "We can have a sponsorship plaque that we give them to hang in their lobbies, and maybe a bigger one here someplace prominent where we add the company names to a list of sponsors for all our guests to see." She realized she had forgotten all about Payson until he laughed.

"Go back to work, Harry. Watch after yourself. Are we still on for Thursday lunch?"

Harriet grinned at him. "Wouldn't miss it. Thanks for checking on me. It was sweet of you."

She waved Payson off and sat down to work on her idea, but a commotion outside of her open lanai doors caught her attention. She walked to the doors, intending to shut them, but was arrested by the sight of two people standing on the beach above the tide line, arguing.

Harriet recognized the slender, red-haired woman immediately. Sequoia Haggedorn still wore her jewels even though she was dressed in a tiny lemon yellow bikini. She stood with her hands on her hips, listening to a man with blonde-tipped blue hair. The man's well-developed chest and massive biceps made Harriet wonder if he was a body builder.

She tried to hear what they were saying, but even though the pair stood near the lanai, the wind was blowing offshore and she couldn't make out the individual words. It was definitely an argument, of that she felt sure, especially when the man grabbed Sequoia's arm and she slapped him.

Harriet was about to go to Sequoia's aid when the young woman threw herself at the man's chest and held onto him. The man's arms went around Sequoia and he patted her back. Harriet stepped back from the open doors before they could realize she'd witnessed their emotional scene. Apparently the man was a friend of Sequoia's and Harriet's concern was misplaced.

She returned to her desk and put in several more hours on her project before deciding to call it a day. Her link buzzed while she was shutting down her computer. Alex's face filled her screen.

"Can you swing by my office on your home?" he asked. "I have some information about Alice Haggedorn I'd like to bounce off you."

"Sure. I was just leaving. Is this a good time?"

"Yep. See you in a few." He cut the connection before Harriet could say goodbye.

She wasted no time clearing her desk, locked the lanai doors, and said a quick goodbye to her parents' holo.

Alex wanted to bounce something off her. Did that mean he valued her opinion? The thought made Harriet's spirits soar. In the six weeks she'd been working at the resort she and Alex had shared dinner twice—once on a date, once pizza at Mermaid Cottage so he could interrogate her about a murder he was trying to solve—one he suspected she'd played a part in.

Alex had also saved her life. And he'd kissed her twice, once after taking her for a ride on his motorcycle at night. A ride under the stars. They had cruised from the mangrove swamp at the island's southern end to the cliffs at the island's northernmost tip where they'd stood watching the phosphorescence in the surf and he'd kissed her. It had been the most romantic experience of Harriet's life.

Since then, nothing. They'd both been busy with the newly opened resort and working every day, often into the evenings.

Harriet was almost to the door that led to the lobby when she realized she was barefoot. She hurried back to her office and dug her heels out from beneath her desk where she'd kicked them off and forgotten about them.

"Stupid heels," she muttered, pulling them on. She really ought to switch to sandals—everyone else working at the resort wore them. But then everyone else wore the resort uniform of khaki pants or shorts with a polo shirt whereas Harriet liked to dress up for work. Once she'd started earning money above and beyond what she needed to live on she had found that she enjoyed wearing nice clothes.

Forced to replace her meager wardrobe after a stalker destroyed her belongings, all the nice clothes she now owned she had bought with Alex advising her. She had tried to ditch him when he invited himself on her shopping trip because he thought she was in danger, but the man proved to be impossible to shake.

He surprised her when she'd learned that he had shopped with his younger sister and actually enjoyed the process. He had even picked things out and sat outside the dressing room ready to critique everything. She had ended up having a fun day with him. The man's sense of style fit well with what she liked to wear. Who'd have guessed?

Harriet had traded the few somber, wool suits and jumpers she'd worn back in Maine for more flattering—and feminine—suits and dresses in silks, rayon, and soft cotton.

Other than the dead bodies she kept finding, her new job was working out better than she had dreamed.

CHAPTER SEVEN

Alex looked over the information that had just come in while he waited for Harriet to arrive. He probably shouldn't have called her but he wanted to see her again. Besides, he wasn't a homicide detective anymore, required to keep the facts of a case to himself. Harriet had a good brain and talking things through with her would help him.

Or so he told himself, knowing full well it was a flimsy excuse to get her alone and spend a little more time with her.

There was still the issue of her lying to him about her past, but he was confident she simply needed to know him better before she felt comfortable enough to share what had to be the most traumatic experience of her life.

He couldn't imagine what it was like for the young Harriet to watch her parents and all her friends die in a mass suicide.

On their only real date he had taken her for a ride on his vintage Triumph Tiger. He could still feel her arms around his waist as she hugged him from behind, her body nestled tight against his back, her joyous laughter in his ear. It had been an experience he hoped to soon repeat.

Mary buzzed him from the lobby and told him that a Miss Monroe was there to see him. Should she let his visitor through?

"I'll be right there, Mary." Alex hurried from the office to meet Harriet at the steel security doors that separated the lobby from the windowless wing that housed two offices, a detention room, a weapons locker, and a hidden lab. The wing was the most secure place on the island and could be accessed only by him, Mary, and one other person.

Alex held open the steel doors that were painted to look like wood and ushered Harriet through, catching the subtle scent of a light lemony soap as she passed by him.

Because of the sensitive nature of his job his office door had automatically locked behind him. He activated the palm security plate and keyed in his code, letting Harriet enter ahead of him.

She set her knapsack on one of two black plastic chairs that sat in front of his desk and looked around. "I see you still haven't done anything with your space," she accused, sliding onto the other chair.

Alex took a minute to look at his work space. No artwork hung on his bare, off-white walls or sat on the shelves filled with forensic manuals and rules and regulation books. There were no holos of family or friends. He kept the few personal items he possessed in his apartment on the second floor.

His office was all business. He liked it that way. Even when he worked on the force he had kept his work space spartan. He didn't like the distraction of the personal to interfere with his work.

Harriet was the most colorful thing in the room. And the most personal. Definitely distracting.

He sat behind his desk, a very large, glossy black affair that dominated the room with its state of the art PC and comm system, its massive surface relieved only by neat stacks of paper.

While most law enforcement workers preferred to receive their reports in digital format, Alex had always preferred paper so he could mark it up and make notes. His former coworkers on the force had teased him about being old-fashioned but he hadn't cared. He had his system and it worked for him.

"What have you learned about poor Mrs. Haggedorn?" Harriet asked as she sat and crossed her legs.

"Several things." Alex forced his gaze away from Harriet's long, shapely legs and pulled a small stack of paper toward him. He read from the top sheet. "Alice Benson married Brian Haggedorn at the tender age of eighteen. They had one child, a son they named Michael, when Alice was twenty. After twenty-two years of marriage Brian died in a boating accident while they were vacationing on the coast of the Dominican Republic."

"Raylene said that Alice told her she grew tired of sitting around her home after she lost her husband. Apparently she liked visiting resorts."

"That corresponds with what I've learned. Alice visited a resort every four months or so for the last ten years." He glanced back at the paper even though he already knew the contents.

"Their son was a ne'er do well, died from drug abuse after a short marriage. One daughter."

"Sequoia Haggedorn. A rather tragic family history."

Alex refrained from pointing out that it wasn't nearly as tragic as Harriet's own family history. It was neither the time nor the place to have that talk.

"As you say." He set down the paper and reached for the second one from the pile. "Sequoia Haggedorn. Age twenty-seven. No permanent relationships on file. Abandoned by her mother after her father's death, went to live with her grandmother. Series of art schools, always quit before graduation, never held a job."

Harriet frowned. "On the surface it sounds as if Sequoia used her grandmother, but we don't know what their relationship was like. Maybe Alice didn't want her granddaughter to work. Maybe

Sequoia likes being a professional student. Did Alice's husband leave her well off?"

"She wasn't filthy rich if that's what you mean, but she was very comfortable. She didn't have to seek work and could afford to travel to spa resorts while maintaining a nice four bedroom condo in New York City."

"Poor Sequoia. She's lost her entire family. Is that all you have?"

"Hardly. Dr. Clarke has already performed the autopsy and was able to put a rush on the lab work. Technically Alice Haggedorn died from heart failure–"

Harriet frowned. "But Dr. Clarke said she was perfectly healthy. She checked Alice out herself. Unless she was negligent how–"

Alex raised a palm toward her. "Let me finish. Alice Haggedorn died from heart failure brought on by an allergic reaction to nicotine."

Harriet stared at him. Real tobacco cigarettes had been hard to come by for decades and were only smoked by the very rich. Most smokers smoked what they called herbals, made from less expensive plants.

"Impossible." She shook her head and frowned. "Dr. Clarke said Alice was a nonsmoker. The lab test must be wrong. Or they've mixed up the results with someone else's test. Even if she did smoke tobacco–and I don't believe that–why did her heart decide to give out this morning? A reaction to nicotine? Impossible," she repeated.

"Alice Haggedorn was not a smoker. You're correct there. Dr. Clarke agreed with you and had the lab run the toxicology tests twice. There's no mistake. Alice Haggedorn died from heart failure brought on by an extreme reaction to nicotine."

Harriet slumped back in her chair. "How? Was she secretly addicted? An addict like her son with nicotine her drug of choice? Did she drink it?"

She pursed her lips and shook her head. "No, that makes no sense. I just don't see it. I can't believe she committed suicide that way. She suffered before she died. If I was going to kill myself I'd want it to be as painless as possible."

Alex was tempted to follow that thought and bring up Harriet's parents but didn't. He wanted Harriet to offer the story when she felt ready. When she trusted him with the truth.

"Why do you assume it was suicide?" he asked instead.

"She was alone in the treatment room, Alex. You said that no one could have snuck in. Even if someone did find a way into Alice's treatment room how could anyone have forced her to take nicotine?"

"Do you remember what she looked like when she came into the spa lobby?"

Harriet thought of the panicked, stumbling woman who had died at her feet that morning. "She was stumbling and breathing hard," she said slowly, recalling the scene. "And her face was hideously swollen. Knowing what I know now I assume that was the nicotine affecting her motor functions. She reached out her hand and asked me to take it, then she collapsed."

"What else?"

"What else? That was the extent of my interaction with her. I can't think of anything else."

Alex sat back in his chair and steepled his fingers. "What did she look like?"

"Besides the bloated face? I couldn't really see her. She had on a robe. It fell open when she fell to the floor. Her face and entire body was covered in green clay."

She stared back at Alex for a few moments before the significance of what she'd told him hit her.

"Oh. The nicotine was in the clay body mask, wasn't it? She absorbed it through her skin. Oh, the poor woman. It wasn't suicide. You had a feeling and you're right. Alice Haggedorn was murdered."

CHAPTER EIGHT

While Harriet felt sorry for the woman who had been murdered, she couldn't help also feeling an acute dismay over the fact that the resort had a second murder to deal with only a few weeks after clearing up the first one.

"Oh no," she said, closing her eyes. "I know you suspected homicide, but I was really, *really* hoping Alice had died from natural causes. The news people are going to have a heyday with this. I can see the headlines now: 'Murder Resort Claims Another Guest'." She opened her eyes and found Alex watching her.

"Sorry," she said flushing. "A moment of self pity. I won't let it happen again. What's next?"

"I need to find out how and when the nicotine was added to Alice Haggedorn's body mask and who had access to it. The list of suspects is small at least. There's only one name on it."

Harriet looked at Alex with horror. "You think Sequoia killed her own grandmother? That's just awful, Alex. Why would she do such a thing?" She pointed to the paper he was still holding. "That makes it sound as if Alice was extremely generous toward her granddaughter. Sequoia is nearly thirty and has never held a job. Her grandmother took her in and has supported her since her mother abandoned her. Alice has treated Sequoia very well."

"Some people want it all, Harriet. Like you said, we don't know what the relationship between Alice and her granddaughter was like. Maybe Sequoia wanted to strike out on her own and Alice wouldn't let her. Maybe Sequoia wanted a large amount of money for some unknown reason and Alice refused to give it to her. Maybe Sequoia is a druggie like her father was."

He shrugged. "The list of reasons people commit murder is fairly short. Money is near the top. While Alice Haggedorn wouldn't be considered an enormously wealthy person by any means, there's enough involved here for it to be a plausible motive."

Harriet stood and wandered around Alex's spartan office but there was nothing to look at to take her mind off the fact that another murder had been committed on the island. He didn't even have a window, she realized with a jolt of surprise. The thick stone walls blocked outside noises. The office was silent except for the sound of her heels as she paced.

She turned and walked back to the desk. "Your office doesn't have a window. I missed that the last time I was in here. Why don't you have a window?"

"Windows can be breached. This wing of the building is the only completely secure area on the island."

Harriet frowned. "I still don't understand. Why is having a secure area necessary?"

"I need a place to safely store weapons or lock someone up if I can't immediately transport them to the police on the mainland."

"You mean like a . . . a murderer?"

"That would be one type of someone, yes."

Harriet decided not to pursue it. She returned the conversation to Alice Haggedorn's murder. "So . . . who are you planning to talk with first?"

"I'm going to start with the spa employees. That's where the murder took place. Somehow, someone knew which treatment room Alice Haggedorn would be in. They also knew that she was going to have the body mask treatment today."

"At the spa you told me and Solly that this was Alice's first time trying the body mask," Harriet said. "She usually got the hot stone treatment. Sequoia talked her into it, I think you said. It doesn't look good for Sequoia, does it?"

"One thing murder detectives try not to do is jump to conclusions. Although even I have to admit that it looks bad for Sequoia since I have no other suspects."

"What about Sequoia's boyfriend?" Harriet asked.

Alex's gaze sharpened. "What boyfriend? There's no mention of a boyfriend in her file, or of her traveling here with anyone other than her grandmother."

"I don't know his name. I saw them together on the beach outside my lanai. The doors were open and I heard them arguing. I went to close the doors and saw them."

"They were arguing?"

"I think so, although I couldn't hear what they were saying so I can't be positive. Judging from Sequoia's body language she seemed upset. It could have been about anything, I suppose. Maybe the boyfriend wasn't being as sympathetic over her grandmother's death as Sequoia thought he should. At any rate they made up. He hugged her and she had her arms wrapped around his waist."

"What did the boyfriend look like?" Alex asked, curious.

"Body builder type. You know, bulging biceps, muscular chest. It looked a little incongruous with his blue hair."

Alex had been taking notes while she spoke. His head snapped up. "Did you say blue hair?"

Harriet nodded. "Yeah. Bright blue with blonde tips. Pretty silly looking."

"Well, well." Alex sat back in his chair and steepled his fingers again.

"Do you know who he is?"

"Yes. Mr. Blue-haired body builder is none other than Terence Leighton, the man who tried to incite a mob in my office lobby earlier."

"What did he do to incite a mob?"

"Accused me of being Mr. Wade's stooge and covering up negligence by the spa staff on Wade's behalf."

"And you let him live?"

The corners of Alex's mouth kicked up into a slow, wolfish grin that showed the dimple in his right cheek.

Harriet's stomach did a little somersault and her pulse quickened. Alex was too attractive for his own good. Or at least too attractive for *her* good.

"He may not live for much longer if he continues to harass me. Now that I know there are two of them . . . well, that makes the murder thing easier to pull off if they're working together."

Harriet nodded toward the sheets of paper near Alex's hand. "Anything on Leighton in there?"

Alex plucked the next sheet off the pile and slid it toward Harriet. She picked it up and skimmed the info. A photo of the blue haired body builder graced the top. It was definitely the same man she'd seen on the beach with Sequoia.

"He's thirty-seven–a full decade older than Sequoia. Half owner of a gym in New York City," she read aloud. "Terence has competed in several body building competitions, never placing higher than fourth place. That's it?"

She slid the paper back toward Alex, noting how he placed it back on the pile and squared the edges. She wondered what his apartment looked like. Was he nasty neat in all areas of his life or just at work? She opened her mouth to ask, then clamped it shut. It was none of her business, although she hoped that someday she'd learn the answer for herself.

"What's next?" she asked instead.

"I think I'll talk to the masseuse who was assigned to Alice

Haggedorn again and get an exact timetable of Alice's movements from the minute she entered the spa. Then I'm going to dig a little deeper into Terence Leighton."

Harriet felt a twinge of disappointment. She had hoped he'd ask her to join him for dinner later. But of course he couldn't spend time socializing with her when he had a murder to solve.

"I guess I haven't been much help." She stood, slung her knapsack over her shoulder, and headed for his door, hoping he hadn't seen her disappointment.

"Yes you have. I didn't know about the boyfriend. That's important information."

Alex came around his desk and joined her, reaching around her for the door switch, standing close enough for Harriet to feel the heat from his body and smell the faint woody muskiness of the soap she associated with him.

"I'll let you get to work," she said, forcing a bright smile.

"I'll walk you out. The steel doors won't open without my palm print and code."

Harriet nodded and followed him down the hall. He opened the steel doors for her but she hesitated on her way through. She was a modern woman. Why couldn't she invite Alex to dinner? Why did the man have to do all the asking?

Before she could voice an invitation, Tarbell Fox appeared from the opposite wing and called to Alex. The opportunity was gone. She felt a curious mixture of disappointment and gratitude over Fox's untimely appearance.

She bid goodbye to both men and consoled herself with the thought that there would be other opportunities.

The problem would be gathering up her courage again.

CHAPTER NINE

Harriet and Solly were running on the beach near their cottages. They often met for a beach run either before or after their work days. Harriet ran barefoot in khaki shorts and a turquoise tank top, her hair caught up in a careless ponytail. Solly wore only his faded jean cutoffs that rode snug on his slim hips and showed off his tanned torso.

The warm, soft breeze had shifted to onshore with the change of the tide and carried the invigorating scent of the ocean. The waves lapped a little more energetically at the white sand as they ate the edges of the island, disappearing in a foamy sizzle as they retreated.

Harriet dodged the hermit crabs carrying their borrowed homes upon their backs as they scurried about looking for edibles washed ashore by the tide. A trio of pelicans coasted by them barely inches above the crests of the waves, their broad wings spread and motionless as they glided. The front bird beat his wings once, twice, then folded them and dove, surfacing a few moments later with a fish in its beak.

"I'm so happy I took this job." Harriet grabbed Solly's hand and squeezed. "This place is truly paradise."

Solly squeezed back and they slowed to a walk. "Even with another dead body? Have you heard if Alex has learned anything yet?"

Harriet immediately felt guilty. Alex had asked her to keep the information he had shared with her to herself. He had trusted her and she couldn't betray that trust, even with her best friend.

She gave Solly a bright, forced smile. She seemed to be smiling that way a lot lately.

"How would I know?" She didn't like keeping a secret from Solly. It made her feel soiled somehow.

"You do know something. I can tell by your voice." Solly jerked playfully on her arm. "Come on, Harry, spill. I'm your best friend, remember? Was the old lady murdered or did she die of natural causes?"

Surely Alex wouldn't mind if she discussed Alice Haggedorn with Solly. He had to realize how close she and Solly were. Besides, Solly was absolutely trustworthy. Still, she hesitated, unsure and feeling caught between her loyalty to her best friend and her promise to Alex.

"Harriet Monroe. I'll tickle it out of you. Come on, tell all. You can't fool me. You know something."

Loyalty to her best friend won out. "Alex asked me not to say anything so you can't repeat this. Alice Haggedorn was murdered."

"Ah, geez. For your sake I was hoping it was a heart attack. How did she die?"

Harriet shook her head and looked out over the water, a picture of Alice's bloated face in her mind. "It must have been awful for her, Solly. Someone spiked her body mask clay with nicotine. The poor woman didn't have a chance once her skin began to absorb the poison. According to Dr. Clarke she had an acute allergic reaction. She must have wondered what was happening to her."

"Murder by nicotine poisoning? That's bizarre." Solly picked up a hermit crab carrying a beautiful brown and white striped shell, waited for him to pop his head back out, and set him back on his way. "Where would anyone even get the stuff? Tobacco is a rich man's item these days, although it used to be fairly common."

"I wouldn't know the first thing about obtaining nicotine. I imagine most people wouldn't either. How did the murderer even come up with the idea?"

Solly turned his head to look at Harriet. "Don't you mean how did Sequoia Haggedorn come up with the idea?"

They stood shoulder to shoulder and watched the sun sinking toward the western horizon. Unlike in Maine, there would be a very short twilight. Once the sun disappeared it would quickly become full dark.

Harriet had been surprised to discover that mornings on the island were the same way. There was a very brief early morning soft gloaming before it became full daylight. Just another aspect of island life that was so very different from her life before.

A wave hit Harriet mid-calf, reminding her that the tide was coming in. It sucked the sand from beneath her feet as it receded, leaving her standing ankle deep in a wet slurry.

"Sequoia is the most logical suspect," she admitted, "but she seemed genuinely upset when she came to pick up her grand-mother. Didn't she?" She turned away from the setting sun and headed for the cottages with Solly's comforting presence at her side.

"Sequoia has a boyfriend," Harriet continued. "At least he appeared to be a boyfriend." She told him about Terence Leighton and Sequoia outside her office and how Terence had brought a mob to the security office.

"Interesting. The plot thickens. You want to have dinner with me so we can talk about it more? One of the chefs gave me his recipe for snapper in coconut sauce and I'm dying to try it. I have everything I need to make it. You bring the wine."

Harriet smiled happily at her friend. "Deal. I'll take a quick shower and join you in, say, thirty minutes?"

"Thirty minutes is not what I call a quick shower," Solly teased, pulling her ponytail. "But sure. See you in thirty."

They parted ways and Harriet hurried into her cottage after hosing the sand from her bare feet. She only needed ten minutes to shower and change but she wanted to do some quick research before dinner.

Solly had raised an interesting question. Where *did* someone obtain a poison like nicotine? She showered, threw on a pair of sweatpants and a short sleeved tee, and quickly braided her hair before sitting down to her PC.

She still didn't have the answer to that question when she let herself into Venus Cottage thirty minutes later, but she knew a lot more about nicotine.

"Did you know that people have been using nicotine as an insecticide since the 1700s?" she asked as she poured and handed Solly a glass of white wine. "But the first known murder using it didn't take place until 1850 in Belgium. A count and his wife wanted her brother's money and poisoned him with distilled nicotine."

"That's harsh. Why are family the ones you have to be most wary of?"

Solomon's cottage was an exact replica of Harriet's with a few differences. The open living space of each was paneled in mahogany, even the ceilings. Tall glass doors in the living space and bedroom faced the sea. Grass mats delineated cozy seating areas.

The kitchen/dining area in both were furnished with high-end appliances. But where Solly's granite counters were a dramatic black, Harriet's were pale rose colored.

Harriet took a seat at the counter and watched Solly heat a pan. He had opened the window shutters, letting the soft evening breeze flow through the cottage. Content, she sipped her wine and let herself relax for the first time since that morning.

Solly had always been more adventurous and entertaining when it came to cooking although she wasn't helpless in the kitchen. After their early years of going hungry and scrounging scraps wherever they could find them, they both had a deep appreciation for good food.

"Get this." Harriet turned her thoughts back to what she'd learned. "Over one hundred years ago, in the early twenty-first century, some supermarket worker poisoned several hundred pounds of ground beef with an insecticide containing nicotine and made more than one hundred people seriously ill.

"Then there was a guy in the late 1990s who murdered his wife by injecting her with nicotine after feeding her sleeping pills. What is wrong with people, Solly?"

Solly looked back over his shoulder at her. "People hurt and kill other people for all sorts of reasons. You know that."

"Alex thinks Alice Haggedorn might have been murdered for money. She's been taking care of Sequoia since Sequoia's mother abandoned her. Alice's son, Sequoia's father, was a junkie and died young. Sequoia has never worked. Ever. She goes to art schools, gets close to graduating and drops out. She's like a . . . a professional student."

"Get the salad. It's in the chiller. Dressing's on the counter. Maybe Sequoia wanted to leave and her grandmother threatened to cut off her funds. If she's never worked then the thought of making it on her own could be scary."

Harriet set the counter and refilled their wine glasses, then sat while Solly served their dinner. They ate in a comfortable and appreciative silence for several minutes.

"This is really good, Sol. Thank your friend for sharing the recipe. And ask him if he minds you sharing it with me, please."

"Doesn't the cook get any credit?" Solly teased.

Harriet lifted her wine glass in a salute. "To the chef. And to–" The door chime sounded before she could finish her toast.

Solly frowned as he slid off his stool. "Who would come calling at the dinner hour?" he grumbled.

Alex's handsome face popped into Harriet's mind. She smoothed a few stray hairs from her face, then felt embarrassed at the vanity and forced herself to pick up her fork and continue eating. She heard a woman's voice in the other room. Not Alex then. How disappointing.

Solly popped his head around the kitchen door frame. "Harry? Can you come out here, please?"

He disappeared before she could ask him who was at the door.

Harriet set down her fork and hurried into the living area. She stopped short when she saw Sequoia Haggedorn standing in the middle of the floor. She had changed from her tiny yellow bikini to a vibrant blue, curve-hugging sheath.

Sequoia wasn't alone. Her blue-haired, body building boyfriend, Terence Leighton, stood beside her. Solly stood behind them, his eyebrows raised in a "what the hell?" expression.

"Harry, you remember Sequoia Haggedorn from the spa this morning? And this is–Terence was it?"

"Yes. Terry Leighton. I'm Sequoia's fiancé."

Fiancé? Harriet schooled her face not to show her surprise. She wondered how long the couple had been affianced and if Alice Haggedorn had known about it.

"I'm pleased to meet you, I'm sure," she said, coolly polite. She looked at Solly, waiting for him to tell her why Alex's prime murder candidates were interrupting their dinner, but she could see he was as puzzled as she was.

"We were just having dinner," Solly said. "Is there something you needed from us?"

Sequoia's smile faltered. "I'm so sorry. We wanted to talk with you about my grandmother's death. You were both at the spa this morning, weren't you? I asked the receptionist–Aaron–and he told me your names."

"We'd only been there for a few minutes before your grand-mother . . . appeared in the lobby," finished Harriet lamely.

"Right. But you were there." Terence Leighton smiled at Harriet. "We need witnesses, you see."

"Witnesses?" Harriet shook her head. "I don't understand. We didn't see–"

Terence didn't let Harriet finish her thought. "We're going to sue the Island Resort for the negligent death of Alice Haggedorn."

"*What?*" Harriet turned wide eyes on Sequoia. *"You're going to what?"*

CHAPTER TEN

"Why would you do that?" Harriet couldn't believe her ears. Sequoia was going to sue the resort? Obviously she didn't realize that Alex had deemed Alice Haggedorn's death a murder.

The four of them stood in Solly's living room. He had not invited Sequoia and her fiancé to take a seat.

"You want to sue the resort?" she repeated, just to make sure.

Sequoia reached for her fiancé's hand. "Yes. Terry thinks that we shouldn't let Douglas Wade get away with the careless way he treats the resort guests." Tears filled her eyes. "My grandmother would still be alive if the spa doctor had done her job properly. We're going to sue her too." She pouted prettily.

Harriet wondered if Sequoia even understand what she was saying. Alice's granddaughter seemed . . . not stupid, but maybe not the brightest bulb on the planet either.

"And we'll sue the big man Wade himself. We'll show him that he can't get away with negligence. We might be nobodies but we aren't afraid of him." Terence puffed up his muscled chest, reminding Harriet of a rooster getting ready to crow.

Where had she ever seen a rooster? Her aunt and uncle had been city dwellers. As a young girl with her parents maybe?

The familiar ache signaling the onset of a migraine started low in her skull. She forced herself to ignore it and focused on the problem at hand.

"Let me be sure I understand you." Solly came around the couple to stand beside Harriet before she could frame another question. "You intend to sue the resort, Dr. Clarke, and Douglas Wade for the wrongful death of Alice Haggedorn."

Terence snapped the fingers of his free hand and pointed at Solly. "Wrongful death. I like it." He repeated the phrase. "Yeah. That sounds like we mean business. That's better than negligent death. We're going to sue for *wrongful death.*"

The shock Harriet had initially felt began to seep away, replaced by anger. She bit her tongue to keep from telling the pair that they were the prime suspects in the murder of Sequoia's grandmother. How dare they talk about suing the resort and Douglas Wade when they were to be blamed?

"I don't see how we can possibly help you," she said, doing an admirable job of hiding her anger. "As I told you, we had only just arrived at the spa. We weren't there even five minutes before your grandmother died."

"Yeah, but you *saw* her die," Terence said, with what sounded suspiciously like relish to Harriet's ears. "You're our key witnesses. You two and Aaron and Raylene. You just have to describe what you saw. How terrible it was. What an awful sight she was when she collapsed. I'll take care of the rest."

He put a protective arm around Sequoia's shoulders. "Don't worry, honey. I've got this." He turned his bright blue eyes on Harriet and Solly.

He was wearing tinted contact lenses. They were a popular enhancement for people who wanted to change their eye color on a temporary basis. Harriet took in the blonde-tipped blue hair and eyes, the body that screamed, "I spend hours in the gym, look at me," and felt a wave of revulsion.

Harriet looked at Sequoia. She was gazing at Terence with

rapt adoration on her face while he squeezed her shoulders and held her curvaceous body tight against his.

"Sequoia." Harriet waited until she had the woman's full attention before continuing. "Are you sure this is what you want? To drag the tragedy of your grandmother's death through the courts? The news media will hound you. You'll be all over the boards and vid screens."

Instead of being dismayed by the thought, Sequoia noticeably brightened. "That's right, we will. Oh, Terry, we'll be on the news! We'll be famous!"

"That's right, baby doll. You can't buy the kind of publicity we'll get. So, you guys in or what? I'm sure we can make sure there's something in it for you, too." He winked at Harriet.

"Yes, well, you do understand that Solomon and I are employees of the resort, right?" She was proud that her voice revealed none of the intense dislike she felt.

Terence misunderstood what she was telling him.

"Don't worry. Not a penny will come out of your pay, I promise. Douglas Wade has the deepest pockets on the planet. What the court awards us won't mean a thing to him. And it's a great opportunity for us. For all of us. If you play your cards right you won't ever have to work again."

Harriet's hand twitched with the effort not to reach out and hurt that smug face in some way. The man was threatening everything she'd worked for and he was telling her she should be grateful? Terence was an asshole of the first order.

"I think you'd better leave," Solly said quietly, and herded them to the door. He practically pushed them out of the cottage and leaned against the door after they'd left.

"Harry! Can you believe that pair? I think you'd better call Alex and let him know what they're up to."

He pushed away from the door and headed for the kitchen. "Unfortunately dinner is ruined. Want more wine instead?"

"Be right back. I left my link in my cottage." Harriet raced next door, retrieved her link, and made it back to Solly's in less than a minute.

"You calling Alex?" asked Solly, handing her a nearly full glass of wine.

"Yes. And then I'm going to call Payson Douglas. He's a close friend of Mr. Wade's and usually knows how to reach him. I think Mr. Wade needs to know what's happening here so he can take steps to stop those two before they create a big media mess."

Harriet placed her calls. Both men wanted to hear the full story in person.

"I'd better open more wine," Solly said after she told him to expect two more guests.

She smiled at her friend's practical nature. He had a way of whittling big problems down to what needed to be done at the moment and not sweating the future. Like eating an elephant one bite at a time, he had told her once.

"I love you, you know," she told him, raising her glass to her lips.

"Love you, too. I couldn't ask for a better friend." Solly smiled at her and took a seat to wait for Alex and Payson.

They had tried once to be more than friends despite Solly's sexual proclivities. It had been a spectacular failure and had reduced both of them to helpless laughter. Fortunately it had also drawn them even closer than they had been before.

Harriet had run away from her aunt and uncle at age fifteen when her uncle began to pay inappropriate and unwanted attention to her and her aunt had refused to believe her, calling her an ungrateful liar.

They'd found each other on the streets of Portland and teamed up, sharing what food and money they could scrape together, sleeping in doorways and abandoned buildings together, protecting each other until Solly had gotten a job and could afford to rent a small room in the slums. They continued to work hard and share as their lives improved. There was no one more important in Harriet's life than her friend Solomon Ayers.

The door chimed, startling Harriet from her thoughts. Alex!

Solly smirked at her as her wine sloshed in her glass. She stuck her tongue out at him and he laughed, then went to answer the door.

Alex could grow to become as important to her as Solly–maybe even more important–she thought suddenly. The knowledge left her feeling a little breathless and not a little stunned.

CHAPTER ELEVEN

"Tell us about your visitors."

Alex had picked up Payson Douglas and brought him to Solly's cottage. Both men accepted glasses of wine and joined them in the living area. Harriet took one cushioned chair and sat with her legs drawn up beneath her. Solly sat on the matching couch with Payson, leaving the chair next to Harriet for Alex.

The men listened carefully as Solly and Harriet took turns relating the story of Sequoia's and Terence Leighton's brief visit. Harriet felt herself becoming angry and annoyed with the couple all over again.

After they'd finished the story Payson took a thoughtful sip of his wine. "You haven't told Sequoia Haggedorn that her grandmother was murdered I take it?" he asked Alex.

"No. I wanted to gather more information on Sequoia first. And after Harriet told me she'd seen Sequoia outside her office with Leighton I thought I'd better check up on him as well."

"Learn anything interesting?" Solly asked.

"A couple things. One, Alice Haggedorn was much more wealthy than I'd originally thought. She sold her husband's company after he died and has invested well. Sequoia is her main beneficiary, but apparently Alice didn't trust her granddaughter's ability to handle money. Upon Alice's death her money flows into a trust with a group of three trustees to handle the investing. Other than a regular monthly draw to cover living expenses and incidentals–a very generous amount I might add–Sequoia has to petition the trustees for any large withdrawals."

"Ouch." Solly grimaced. "That sounds a little harsh. How old is Sequoia? Thirty? And her grandmother didn't trust her with money?"

Harriet remembered the way Sequoia had leaned on Terence Leighton, trusting him to take care of everything. She'd bet her next month's pay that Terence was a fortune hunter, the very type of man Alice Haggedorn wanted to protect her granddaughter from.

"I don't think it was a matter of trust," she said slowly. "I think it was more that Alice was worried about fortune hunters getting their hands on Sequoia's inheritance and blowing through it."

She looked at Alex. "I got the impression that Sequoia may not be bright enough to handle large amounts of money. And she may not be a very good judge of character, especially if she's agreed to marry Terence Leighton. And come to think of it, I'm not even sure she's intelligent enough to come up with such a diabolical way to murder someone. She comes across as . . . innocent and a bit childish to me."

"Point taken," Alex said. "I only spoke with Sequoia briefly at the spa and of course she was crying and upset. It was hard to get a good read on her other than she loved her grandmother–or at least acted as if she loved her."

"I did some quick research on nicotine poisoning," Harriet told them. "It isn't easy to come up with liquid nicotine. You need a large quantity of leaves and a way to distill it."

"Or if they know someone on the black market they could have bought the nicotine already distilled," Solly pointed out.

Harriet watched Alex make a note to check out black market

sources, then told them about the few historic nicotine poisoning cases she'd found where murder had been intended and successfully committed. When she fell silent they all sat quietly, thinking and sipping wine.

She felt relaxed and comfortable, Harriet realized. Like they were all friends. The thought warmed her.

"Have you had a chance to investigate the fiancé yet?" Payson asked Alex. "What's his name? Terence Leighton?"

"Yes, and he's a good candidate for a fortune hunter. He's just become full owner of a gym that isn't doing very well and he's accumulated a large pile of debt. His ex-partner in the gym says Leighton wanted too much too fast. He borrowed to add a fancy spa onto the gym when he should have waited until they had turned a profit before sinking more money into the business. The partner refused to go along with the expansion and forced Leighton to buy him out."

"So you're saying that Leighton is desperate for money." Solly raised his eyebrows at Alex. "Desperate enough to murder an innocent old woman for it?"

"Maybe."

Payson set his wine glass on the coffee table and leaned back. Harriet debated asking him whether Douglas Wade would make a trip to the resort in light of this new trouble–she was curious to meet the man who had hired her–but decided it was really none of her business. If Mr. Wade valued his privacy as much as he seemed to then she would honor that.

"What else have you learned, Alex?" Payson asked. "Do you know yet how the nicotine was added to the body mask?"

"Alice Haggedorn's masseuse, Nakeesha Bain, told me that Alice insisted on using the same treatment room and masseuse for each of her visits. According to Nakeesha Alice didn't like different strangers working on her body. She preferred to get comfortable with one space and one masseuse. Nakeesha was happy to oblige. She liked Mrs. Haggedorn, called her a spunky old lady."

"Huh. That's how Raylene, the receptionist, described Alice too." Harriet looked at Alex. "So you think someone knew which room Alice would be using and snuck in while no one was looking. Why didn't Nakeesha suffer from the effects of the nicotine? Her hands must have absorbed it when she applied it to Alice's body."

"She wore gloves, she told me, because the clay dries out her hands too much, especially if she does several body masks a day." Alex shrugged. "Makes sense. Her hands are her living. I don't think she's involved at all."

"Could someone else who works there have added the nicotine to the mask?" Harriet set her wine glass on the coffee table next to Payson's. She'd had enough to drink. She felt overtired and stressed and the wine had hit her harder than she liked. She didn't want to trigger a migraine.

Alex wagged a hand back and forth. "Anything's possible, I suppose. Whether it's likely or not is another matter. I haven't run a thorough check on the spa employees other than Nakeesha. I suppose if one was in need of money then Sequoia or Terence could have paid them to add the nicotine."

"They might not have even realized that what they were adding was a poison," Harriet said. She hated to think that a spa employee could be paid to commit murder. She warmed to her theory. "What if Sequoia told the person that it was an essential oil of some kind to help with her grandmother's arthritis. Or rheumatism, or whatever."

"Not bad."

Harriet basked under Alex's approving look. Then she remembered the sight of Alice Haggedorn dying and felt ill. "Everyone seemed to like her. And now she's dead because someone wanted her money. It's not right."

"The world is full of scum," Payson said quietly. "I'm sorry it has to touch the resort. It's not what this place is about."

"Will Mr. Wade fight Terence Leighton's efforts to sue him and the resort?" Harriet gave Payson an anxious look.

Payson waved off her concern. "Trust me, Terence Leighton is nothing. Wade has dealt with much more savvy and ruthless con men. He'll be more concerned with getting justice for Alice Haggedorn."

"Con man?" Solly raised his eyebrows. "You're right. I wonder if that's exactly what this is. One big con. Leighton wants to get his hand into Wade's deep pockets–he even said as much. Let's say that he doesn't care about Sequoia's inheritance because he knows he can't get his hands on the trust. But he *can* make a lot of trouble for the resort and Mr. Wade with bad publicity. He might not even want to actually sue–that will cost him money for lawyer's fees. He might be angling for a big settlement to keep quiet instead. Hoping the threat is enough to make Wade pay up."

"We need more facts." Alex stood. "I'm going to go back to my office and dig deeper into everyone involved. I can tap a source with ties to the black market to see if I can get a line on how someone would obtain liquid nicotine."

Payson stood as well. "Don't get up you two. We'll see ourselves out." He took Harriet's hand and squeezed it. "Try not to worry too much, my dear. Wade can look after himself and he isn't about to let some young punk hurt the resort. Tomorrow's Thursday. Are we still on for lunch?"

Harriet smiled. "I wouldn't miss it. Please tell Mr. Wade that we'll do everything we can to help him."

Payson's pale blue eyes twinkled. "I will. I'm sure he appreciates your loyalty and commitment to the resort."

After the two men left Harriet helped Solly clean up the dinner dishes. They sat on the lanai and opened another bottle of wine–she decided she hadn't had too much after all–and watched the stars and sparkling bright green phosphorescence on the waves as they rolled in to the shore.

"Island night music."

"What?" She could just make out Solly's eyes shining in the dark.

"Listen." A light breeze rattled the palm fronds in the half dozen trees that flanked Solly's cottage. Insects buzzed. A night bird raised its voice in song, then fell silent. The waves lapped softly at the beach in front of them.

"Island night music," she echoed softly.

She was happy here. Happier than she'd ever been anywhere else she could remember. She couldn't remember her life before the death of her parents other than brief snatches of memory. Those brief glimpses all *seemed* happy, but she couldn't remember enough to even put together a remembered event or conversation.

She wished she could remember more.

CHAPTER TWELVE

"Ms. Monroe, there's a Mr. Leighton here to see you."

Harriet looked at Jeeves's face in her office link and tried to hide her surprise. Terence Leighton was here? And he wanted to see her? She looked around her lovely office and realized she didn't want his presence to taint her beautiful work space.

"Tell him I'll be right out, Jeeves, thank you."

Whatever Sequoia's boyfriend wanted had to be bad for the resort.

She slipped on her heels, vowing once again to buy several pairs of practical sandals next time she was on the mainland, and made her way out to the lobby.

Terence Leighton was indeed there, posing in front of the windows in a chest hugging sleeveless tank and snug shorts that left little to the imagination. He turned when he heard the door slide shut behind her and smiled.

"*Harry,* I'm so glad I caught you." He rushed across the lobby, grabbed Harriet's hand, and tried to pull her in for a hug.

Harriet put up her elbow, catching him in the stomach and pulled away. She tried to free her hand but he kept a tight hold on it. She glared at Terence but he was either ignorant or ignoring her.

"It's Miss Monroe. What can I do for you, Mr. Leighton?" she asked through clenched teeth. The idiot was crushing her hand.

"Oh, but your friends call you Harry. I asked around. And you must call me Terry. All my friends do." He gave her a conspiratorial wink.

"We aren't friends, Mr. Leighton." Harriet tugged harder and freed her hand.

"But we will be. I'm here to do you a favor, Harry. A *big* favor."

Harriet raised her eyebrows but decided fighting the familiar use of her name was pointless–Terence Leighton wasn't hearing a word she said.

"You want to do me a favor? What kind of favor?" Was he about to offer her money to lie about the spa? She felt her temper rise and clenched her jaw.

Terence beamed at her and spread his hands as if he was about to bestow a benediction upon her. "I'm going to make you famous, Harry. You'll be all over the news feeds by this time tomorrow."

"*What?*" Harriet couldn't keep the horror she felt from her voice or her face. "Why would I be on the news?"

Leighton's chest puffed up. "Because I've invited the top reporters to come here and interview you live. Along with me and Sequoia of course. It *is* our story after all. But you'll feature in it, I promise," he added as the look of horror on Harriet's face deepened.

Terence Leighton had invited reporters to the resort to interview her? "Will they be interviewing the others from the spa as well?"

"Oh yes." Terence rubbed his thick palms together. "We'll all be famous, at least for our fifteen minutes, eh?" He winked again.

Harriet noticed that the man's buffed and bronzed skin had zero body hair. Did he shave it all off or wax it? Maybe he'd had full-body electrolysis. That would have cost a fortune. But then, he was angling to get himself a fortune without actually earning one, wasn't he? And why was she thinking about something so inconsequential as body hair when disaster surely loomed?

Harriet didn't bother to try hiding the disgust she felt as she turned away. "Jeeves, Mr. Leighton is leaving. Would you please help him out the door and make sure he doesn't return."

She turned back to the puzzled man beside her as Jeeves came around his counter. "Jeeves will help you out, Mr. Leighton." She had no qualms about setting the droid on Terence Leighton. Even a body builder's muscles were no match for the superior strength of a droid.

Harriet watched Jeeves propel the bewildered Terence out of the office. "Are you all right, Miss Harry?" he asked when he returned. Always proper and correct, Jeeves only used her more familiar nickname in private, and only after she'd insisted that he do so, but he still couldn't drop the formal 'Miss'.

"I'm sorry I allowed him in to see you. He checked out as a guest so I had no idea–"

Harriet held up a hand. "It wasn't your fault, Jeeves. There's no way you could have known. The man may be a guest but he's trying to cause trouble for the resort. If he returns call Alex, will you please?"

"Sure thing, Miss Harry. I promise you he won't get back in."

Jeeves let her back through the door that led to the offices. Harriet wasted no time getting Alex on the link and telling him that Terence Leighton had invited reporters to the island for interviews.

"We'll see about that," Alex said grimly. "Thanks for the heads up." He broke the connection.

Harriet paced her office for several minutes while she tried to think of something that would counteract the bad publicity Sequoia and her fiancé were about to generate. Unfortunately, bad publicity seemed inevitable.

Even if the pair was arrested later and charged with murder, there would be fallout. The news media fed on stories like the murder of Alice Haggedorn. The more sensational the better. And any story even remotely connected to the richest man on the planet would give it extra juice and guarantee plenty of air time. There was nothing she could do to stop it.

Her comm buzzed again, interrupting the downward spiral of her thoughts.

"Payson Douglas is here for your lunch date, Miss Monroe."

Harriet brightened. Lunch with Payson was just the antidote she needed after her brief encounter with Terence Leighton. "I'll be right out."

She checked that the lanai doors were locked before heading back to the lobby to meet her standing Thursday lunch date. They walked together over to the employee dining room and were soon seated outside at a semi-private table under a vine-covered trellis.

Large drooping clusters of purple and white fragrant flowers hung from the vines and protected the outdoor seating from the hot sun. Small colorful birds and geckos flitted through the vines searching for bugs. Harriet could hear the quiet murmur of conversation from the other employees taking their midday meal.

It felt exactly like every other lunch date she'd enjoyed with Payson. She took a sip of her pineapple drink and relaxed slightly. This was just what she needed to get her mind off Sequoia and her troublemaking fiancé.

"I wasn't sure you'd have time for an old man today," teased Payson after they'd given the waitress their orders.

"Why wouldn't I?"

"I'm sure you've been wracking your brain trying to come up with a way to neutralize any negative publicity Sequoia Haggedorn and her fiancé might generate over the unfortunate death of

Alice Haggedorn. Be honest with me now. You have, haven't you?"

Harriet blushed but couldn't help laughing. "Yes. I admit it. It just seems grossly unfair, Payson. The resort is so lovely, and everyone who comes here has a wonderful time and vows to return. A few rotten souls shouldn't be allowed to ruin it for everyone else."

Payson cocked his head and looked at her. "Has something else happened that I haven't heard about? You seem . . . more worked up than you were last night."

"I guess I'm still mad at Terence Leighton. He came by my office shortly before you arrived to tell me that he's invited a bunch of reporters to the resort and they're going to interview the spa employees–and him and Sequoia, of course. He wanted to let me know that the reporters want to interview me as well but I asked Jeeves to toss him out on his ear."

She sighed. "I probably shouldn't have done that. It will just make him dig in his heels more."

"Hmmm. We'll see about that. Excuse me a moment, Harry." Payson pulled his link from his pocket.

"Alex? Have you heard about Leighton's latest?" He listened for a moment. "All taken care of? Good."

Payson pocketed his link. "No reporters will be coming to the island, Harry. Only resort shuttles are allowed to land here anyway. If any others try they'll be turned away. We protect the privacy of our guests, as you know. Wouldn't do to have photographers with telescopic lenses taking pictures of them while they try to relax and get away from the pressures of their lives."

The waitress brought their lunches before Harriet could think of an appropriate response.

Payson smiled at her and picked up his fork. "Relax and enjoy your lunch, my dear. The problem is under control. Now, tell me more about your plan to bring underprivileged children to the island."

They didn't have long to enjoy their meal. Halfway through there was a disturbance in the dining room, followed shortly by the appearance of Sequoia Haggedorn, wearing a bright purple bandeau top and a lime skirt that barely covered the cheeks of her ass.

Sequoia looked around the tables until she spied Harriet, then stomped over to her and stopped with her hands on her hips. "You're trying to ruin my chance to avenge my Gamma's death," she accused.

"*What?* Are you *mad?*" Harriet was beginning to really dislike Sequoia Haggedorn.

Sequoia pointed a multi-ringed hand at her and tossed her head. Harriet saw that she still wore the ruby in her navel. How did she get it to stay there? Was it permanently affixed with some type of glue?

And why was she thinking about such an unimportant thing when she had real trouble threatening her? She'd done the same thing with Terence Leighton. Was she losing her ability to focus? She forced herself to tune back into Sequoia's tirade.

"Terry told me about how you refuse to tell the reporters the truth. We'll find a way. You can't stop us." Sequoia's voice vibrated with righteous indignation. "And when we do the resort and Mr. Wade will pay through the nose. That's what Terry says. *Through the nose!*"

She had bent forward almost until her own nose touched Harriet's. Harriet's hands twitched with the urge to reach up and grab the woman's perfect pert nose and twist, but she resisted. She didn't want to embarrass Payson by creating any more of a scene. The other diners had fallen silent and she could see curious faces turned their way.

"Would you like a seat, ma'am?" Payson stood and held a chair out for Sequoia.

"Oh." Sequoia straightened and smiled sweetly at Payson. "No, thank you, I just had lunch."

Sequoia couldn't have been as upset as she acted if she was able to eat lunch, Harriet observed drily. When was Alex going to tell them that her grandmother had been murdered? It was the only way to stop the pair from their bogus crusade.

Sequoia's expression grew angry again as she turned away from Payson to look at Harriet. "We're not done with you," she said, and sashayed back into the dining room.

Harriet and Payson both watched her leave.

"I do believe that woman could be dangerous," Payson murmured. "You'd better watch your back, my dear."

CHAPTER THIRTEEN

It had been a crappy day, starting with the morning encounter with Terence Leighton. Her Thursday lunch date had started well, but despite Payson's efforts to get her to eat, Harriet had been unable to finish her lunch after Sequoia's grand exit from the employee dining room.

The afternoon had spiraled downward from there with a frantic visit from the resort manager. The news hounds had been alerted and were hot on the scent of scandal at the fabulous Island Resort. It didn't help that any story linked to the reclusive Douglas Wade made the world sit up and take notice.

Cassie's link was buzzing non-stop. She'd finally fled to Harriet's office, but there'd been little Harriet could say to help.

It was enough to make Harriet feel sick with impotence, a feeling she'd experienced only once before–shortly before she'd run away from her aunt and uncle. Then at least she had been able to come up with a plan–even if it was only to run away.

Unfortunately that plan wouldn't work for her now. She paused, oblivious to the large blue and green lizard watching her from the undergrowth beside the road. Hadn't she also run away from her ex-fiancé less than two months before? Was that her default method for dealing with problems?

No. She wouldn't believe that about herself. Her Aunt Wendy accused her of lying when she tried to tell her that Uncle Arthur was making sexual advances toward her. And her ex had been obsessive and wouldn't let her go. Running away had been her only option in both those situations.

Not this time. This time she would find a way to help the resort. This time there would be no running.

She let herself into Mermaid Cottage, tossed her knapsack onto a chair, and went to stand in front of the lanai doors where she stared out at nothing. The sight of the white beach and turquoise water that usually filled her with happiness barely registered on her busy mind.

What was she going to do?

She was the resort's Public Relations Director. It was her responsibility—and no one else's—to find a way through the mess that Terence Leighton and Sequoia Haggedorn were creating. Unfortunately she had nothing to work with. She didn't know how to neutralize the bad press they were bringing to the resort.

Her only hope was for the pair to be charged with murder. Then *that* would fill the headlines, not the resort's negligence.

The resort hadn't been negligent. *That* was what frustrated her so. Someone had added nicotine to Alice Haggedorn's body mask knowing that it would most likely kill her. Or at the very least they hoped to make her deathly ill so the next attempt would succeed.

Was that what the original plan had been?

Harriet turned away from the doors and hurried over to her desk. Smaller than her rosewood office desk and built from cherrywood, the desk was still large enough to serve as her home office space if she needed to bring work home. She fired up the PC and brought up her research on nicotine poisoning.

There! The man who had injected a lethal dose into his wife

while she lay paralyzed by sleeping pills had dosed her with smaller amounts several times previously. When the wife became ill each time the husband took her to the hospital. The doctors couldn't make any sense of her symptoms and diagnosed an unknown illness. By the time he administered the final, lethal dose they assumed the mysterious illness killed her.

Harriet drummed her fingers on the desktop. Had the original plan been to simply make Alice Haggedorn ill? Maybe they'd been setting the stage for a later murder and they had miscalculated the dose. She could easily imagine both Sequoia or Terence messing up the dosage.

But what if their plan had been to make Alice ill and then blame the resort? If Alice hadn't experienced an allergic reaction and died the nicotine wouldn't have been found and questioned. Sequoia and Terence could have claimed that the spa caused her illness somehow and then tried to extort money from the resort for emotional trauma or some similar bull crap.

She had no doubts that money was at the root of the poisoning.

The door chime interrupted Harriet's thoughts. She powered down the PC and went to see who was calling but hesitated before opening the door. What if it was Sequoia or Terence Leighton, or god forbid–both of them?

The door chimed again. She reached for the doorknob but still hesitated.

"Harriet? It's Alex. Are you in there?"

Harriet felt a rush of relief at the sound of Alex's deep voice. She yanked the door open and barely refrained from throwing herself at him.

"Alex. I thought you might be Sequoia or her fiancé. I'm ashamed to admit I was afraid to open the door."

"Payson called me. I don't blame you one bit for being cautious. He told me about your lunch date." Alex glanced over the door. "I'll get a security cam installed tomorrow so you'll know who's out here before you let them in. We didn't think that peepholes or cams would be needed on the employee cottages, altho we installed peepholes in all the employee apartment doors. Looks like I'll have to rethink that. May I come in?"

Harriet stepped back to let him inside and closed and locked the door after him. "I'm feeling a little paranoid," she said when he raised his eyebrows at her.

"Even with me here? Never mind. It's understandable. Why don't you change out of your work clothes and take a walk on the beach with me? I've been cooped up all day and could use some fresh air and sunshine. I imagine you could too."

Harriet's mood brightened. "I'd love to."

"I like that dress by the way," he called after her as she left to change. "It's one of my favorites."

The dress was one of Harriet's favorites too. A lightweight, sleeveless rose silk that skimmed her upper body and flared at the hips, it was one that Alex had chosen for her when he helped her replace her damaged wardrobe. She had chosen it that morning because it made her feel confident whenever she wore it and because of her lunch date with Payson, who always looked elegant no matter what he wore.

Who would have guessed that a tough, ex-New York City murder detective would have great fashion sense?

Alex wandered over to Harriet's display of hand-carved wooden hippos and idly picked one up. He didn't know the names of the exotic woods but he bet Harriet could name every one of them.

The hippos were important to her, he knew. Her friend Solomon had given her one for her birthday one year, a big splurge for a poor young man since wood was extremely expensive and hard to come by. And for every birthday after that Solomon had gifted Harriet a new and different hippo.

Unfortunately a stalker had destroyed Harriet's collection soon after she arrived on the island. Douglas Wade had generously replaced them—and added a few new additions. Even Alex could see that each one was finely detailed and exquisitely carved.

"They aren't exactly the same as the ones Solly gave me but I still love them." Harriet came to stand beside Alex and picked up a tiny baby hippo with a gaping wide mouth. She ran a finger over its smooth back and set the hippo back with its mother. "You ready? I'll grab my bag and a couple of waters for us."

Alex gave Harriet an assessing look. She had changed into long khaki shorts and a pale blue tee shirt that showed off the light tan she'd acquired since moving to the island. Her thick honey-colored hair had been pulled back into a careless ponytail. He could see that the skin around her eyes looked tight and slightly bruised, an indication of the strain she was feeling.

"I'm more than ready," he said. "Lock up behind you. I'll wait on the beach."

The fresh air and soothing sound of the advancing and retreating waves began working their magic on Harriet. She felt the tension begin to seep from her body as they walked.

They had walked far beyond the cottages before Alex spoke again. "Feeling any better?"

Harriet smiled and nodded.

"Good. Now tell me about Sequoia's visit to the employee dining hall." Alex listened without interrupting her.

"Why haven't you charged them with Alice's murder yet?" Harriet asked.

"First, I can't charge them because I'm no longer a cop. Second, I can't call in the police and have them charged without proof of some sort. I need at least reasonable cause to get a search warrant for their rooms. I don't have it."

Harriet turned her head sharply at the frustrated tone of Alex's voice. She and Cassie weren't the only ones affected by Terence Leighton and Sequoia Haggedorn. Alex had a murdered woman on his hands and no longer had the authority of a badge.

With the security of the resort resting on his broad shoulders he had to miss the power of a badge.

She took a deep breath and let it out. "This is so frustrating. We know Alice was murdered. Who else would want her dead but her granddaughter and the money hungry fiancé?"

"No one that I can see. The problem is that I can't figure out how the nicotine was added to the clay body mask. Unless I can come up with a way that either Sequoia or Leighton used to put the nicotine in the mask–" he ran one hand through his dark hair. "I've got nothing. I have to know how it was done."

Harriet took Alex's free hand in sympathy and they walked hand in hand without speaking until they reached the mangrove swamp at the southern tip of the island. Alex sat on a large root at the edge of the beach and pulled Harriet down onto the space beside him.

She sat, and tried not to blush at the feel of his bare, muscled thigh pressed against her leg. His skin felt warm and slightly rough against hers and sent a warm glow spreading through her body.

He released her hand and circled her shoulders with his arm, drawing her against him. "I won't let anything happen to you, Harriet. You can trust me on that."

Harriet sighed. She felt so safe with Alex. Had she ever felt this safe?

"I don't think Sequoia and Terence Leighton are really dangerous in that they'd try to physically hurt me," she said slowly. "They're just a lot of trouble. Trouble for the resort, which means trouble for me. And you. And Cassie. And Mr. Wade."

"Nonetheless, Sequoia threatened you today. I don't intend to let her or her muscle bound boyfriend get near enough to hurt you. I want you to let me stay at the cottage with you until this is over."

Harriet's stomach somersaulted. Alex sleeping in her living room? Or–she could barely breath thinking about it–in her bed?

It would be like living together. *They would be living together.* And afterward? He'd leave a big, empty space when he left. Would she be able to deal with that? She suspected she was already half in love with Alex Hayes. It wouldn't take much to push that over to all the way in love.

Before she could answer, Alex gently took her chin, tipped her head up and lowered his lips to hers, kissing her softly at first, then more insistently. Harriet opened her lips for him and tasted him with her tongue. He groaned and wrapped both of his arms around her, deepening the kiss even further.

Harriet's arm circled Alex's neck and she threw herself into the kiss. Bradley Higgins, her ex and the only other man she'd ever kissed–other than trying it once with Solly–had never kissed her like this. She felt exhilarated and wonderful.

A warm ache moved into her breasts and through her lower body. Yes! This was how being kissed was supposed to feel.

Alex drew his head back and kissed Harriet's eyelids and temples. "You are quite beautiful you know."

Harriet laughed. She felt a little lightheaded and not quite herself. "Right." She tapped the bump on her prominent nose. "Not with this honker, I'm not. But thank you for saying it. It is very gallant of you."

She became aware of the shallow sun warmed water lapping at her ankles. Hermit crabs searched her toes, tickling her with their tiny claws. Frogs croaked deeper in the swamp and birds sang and called. The breeze turned and she could smell the sulfurous, rotten egg smell from the swamp. She didn't care. At that moment the mangrove swamp felt like the most romantic place on the planet.

Alex ran his finger gently down the length of her nose, tapping the bump. He rubbed his thumb over her swollen lips.

"You are beautiful," he repeated, and kissed her again.

Harriet closed her eyes against the tears that threatened to fall. Nobody had ever told her that she was beautiful before. It made her ache with a longing she couldn't quite name.

"I want you to trust me." Alex took each of her hands in his own strong hands and squeezed gently to emphasize his words. His deep blue eyes were steady on hers. "I want you to be able to talk to me about anything. Anything at all. I will never hurt you, Harriet. I promise."

"Thank you." Harriet's words were barely above a whisper. She made an effort to find her voice. "I do trust you, Alex."

"Good." He stood and pulled Harriet to her feet. "Let's go back to Mermaid and get something to eat. Invite Solomon over. Maybe between the three of us we can figure out how the nicotine was added to Alice Haggedorn's body mask. Lord knows I can use all the help I can get."

The trip back to Harriet's cottage took less time than the one to the swamp. They talked very little. Harriet couldn't shake the feeling that she had missed something important in Alex's words.

Unfortunately she had no clue what that was.

CHAPTER FOURTEEN

The next morning Tarbell Fox picked up Alex, Solomon, and Harriet and drove them all to the spa. True to his word that he intended to protect her, Alex had camped on Harriet's living room floor. Unbeknownst to her, he had shown up prepared with a camp pad and a sleeping bag as well as a duffle of clothing and bathroom essentials.

Harriet felt both relieved and slightly frustrated that he made no overture toward joining her in her king-size bed which was foolish because what would she have said or done if he had?

She honestly didn't know. And that right there told her she wasn't ready. Apparently Alex knew her better than she did.

Outside Mermaid cottage Alex sat in the passenger seat of the four-wheel drive, hydrogen powered vehicle known as the Road Hog with his assistant and forced himself to think about the day ahead. Sleeping on the floor while he knew Harriet was asleep in the next room had been more difficult than he'd anticipated.

He'd slept in fits and starts, and whenever he woke he thought about going to her. He felt confident that he could seduce her. But he'd stopped himself. He wanted more than a physical relationship with Harriet. Sex was easy to come by. He'd never had a problem finding willing partners.

But even before coming to the island Alex had known that sex was no longer enough for him. He wanted to feel intimately connected to one special woman. He wanted the whole enchilada. And from the moment he'd laid eyes on her he'd known that he wanted it with Harriet Monroe.

Until she trusted him enough to tell him the real story about her parents' death they'd never be able to achieve that.

"We're here, Boss. The equipment you asked for is in the back."

Alex pushed away his brooding thoughts and climbed out of the Road Hog.

"What equipment?" Harriet asked, exiting the backseat with Solly.

"Alex asked for climbing gear and a few other things," Fox answered as he joined Alex at the rear of the Hog and grabbed a duffle. "What's next?" he asked Alex.

"Next we see if we can figure out how someone spiked Alice Haggedorn's body mask with nicotine."

The two men entered the spa with Harriet and Solomon at their heels.

Harriet felt the peaceful serenity of the spa as soon as she walked through the door. Whale song and ocean waves flowed softly from hidden speakers. Aaron and Raylene were behind the desk working their PCs. The waterfall wall flowed softly into the waterlily and koi pond.

Raylene looked up from her task and smiled at the group before hurrying around the counter and positively beaming at Alex. "Alex! How can I help you this morning?"

Harriet refrained from rolling her eyes. She'd heard rumors that nearly every female on the island had been trying to hook up with Alex since his arrival. She had even had an unpleasant experience with one who thought Harriet was trying to take him away from her.

Apparently even a woman as young as Raylene wasn't immune to Alex's charms. Harriet saw Aaron shoot Alex a dirty look and wondered if he was jealous. She recalled the way Aaron had consoled the female receptionist on the day of the murder and thought he probably was jealous.

"We'll be in Alice Haggedorn's treatment room, Raylene. Please see that we aren't disturbed." Alex headed for the hallway behind the waterfall wall, leaving a crestfallen Raylene behind.

Two minutes later the four of them stood inside the scene of Alice Haggedorn's murder. Signs of fingerprint powder still remained. Harriet noted with interest that there were insect tracks in the dust on the counter that held the mask heater. Palmetto bugs? Impossible to keep them out with a wall that was wide open to the jungle.

Fox and Alex set down the duffles and walked to the edge of the open wall.

"Okay, here's what we have." Alex stood with his hands in his pockets and pursed his lips, looking out over the lush growth that sloped away from the rear of the spa. "As I see it, *if* the murderer entered the room from the jungle then the only tree he could have used would be *that* one."

He pulled his right hand from its pocket and pointed to a tall coconut palm that stood about five feet from the edge of the room's floor.

Harriet joined them, careful to keep back from the very edge of the drop-off. She craned her neck to see the base of the tree. "That looks like quite a climb," she observed. "Can it be done?"

Alex looked at her. "We're going to find out. Fox, do you want the honors or shall I?"

Harriet looked at Fox's burly body and frowned. The men and boys she'd observed climbing the island's coconut palms were slim and lithe. Neither Alex nor Fox fit that description.

Fox's bright green eyes sparkled beneath his short red hair. "Tough choice, boss. I'm not sure either of us are built to climb that tree."

Both men turned to look at Solomon who was slimmer than either of them. When they smiled Harriet knew that they had planned this ahead of time.

"I'd love to give it a shot," Solly said immediately. "I'd hate to let you two have all the fun."

Harriet kept quiet. She knew that Solly's looks were deceiving. He had become hooked on climbing walls and obstacle courses once he was making enough money to afford a yearly gym membership. Consequently her friend was much stronger than he looked.

Fox grabbed one of the duffles and he and Solomon headed out of the building. Several minutes later they reappeared at the base of the palm. Fox pulled a special climbing apparatus made especially for the branchless palms from the duffle and handed Solly a pair of leather gloves.

Harriet watched with interest as Fox attached a small flat platform to the palm's trunk with a thick length of webbing. Solly stood on the platform and Fox strapped it to his feet, checking that they were secure. Fox then hooked another webbing strap to a harness around Solly's waist, ran it around the tree, and attached the free end to the other side of Solly's waist.

After another few minutes passed while Solly worked out the proper method to slide the waist strap up the trunk, use it to hold his body in place, and then lift the foot platform. Soon Solly was making his way toward them.

"That doesn't look easy," Harriet remarked. "And it's noisy. It would be impossible to sneak up on anyone in this room."

"I agree. Be right back." Alex turned and left the room.

Harriet watched Solly make his laborious way up the smooth trunk. He was breathing hard but grinning in triumph when he reached the level of the spa. Harriet looked up. The palm easily extended another forty feet above them.

Solly followed her gaze. "Phew! This is harder than it looks. I have developed a sudden admiration for anyone who climbs these suckers."

"I could easily see you climbing from the room on either side of this one," Alex said as he rejoined Harriet. "If anyone entered the spa from this direction to poison the body mask they would have had to do it before the spa opened."

"Which is a possibility," Solly pointed out. "Shall I see if I can make the leap from here to there?"

Harriet's mouth dropped open in horror. "Solly, no! If you fell you'd break every bone in your body."

But Solly wasn't listening to her. He'd unhook the webbing strap from his waist and leaned down to unstrap his feet, one arm wrapped around the palm's trunk to keep from falling. He stood carefully, still hanging on.

"Ready?" he asked Alex. "I really don't fancy climbing back down the tree. You're going to catch me if I don't quite make it, right?"

Harriet noticed then that Alex had also donned gloves. Her eyes widened. "You're serious? But–"

Solly didn't give her time to finish her thought. He flexed his knees and leaped, landing on the very edge of the room. Alex grabbed him as Solly windmilled his arms and began to tilt backwards.

"Thanks. Obviously I need to bone up on my broad jump skills," Solly said, grinning.

Harriet punched her friend on the arm. "How could you? Damn you, you could have died, Solly. Don't ever do that again."

"It had to be done, Harry." Solly rubbed his arm. "If Alex can't figure out how they put the nicotine in the mask Sequoia and her blue haired boyfriend are going to get away with killing an innocent woman."

"How'd it go?" Tarbell Fox joined them and clapped Solly on the back. "I was glad you made the leap, man. You had me crapping my drawers for a second there."

"It could be done," Alex said, "but it's highly unlikely this is *how* it was done. The leap across from the palm tree to the room isn't easy and Terence Leighton is muscle bound. Even Solly with his long legs almost didn't make it. I think we can safely rule this out."

"Want me to jump back onto the tree?"

Alex grinned then. "Nah, we can unhook the equipment from here."

Fox pulled a telescoping pole from the second duffle and proceeded to free the equipment. It fell to the ground with a soft thud. "All right, first method shot down. Let's try theory number two."

They spent the next hour trying various methods for entering the three sided room. Climbing over or under the walls that extended four feet beyond the edge of the floor left obvious tell-tale marks on the wall's surface. Same with trying to climb beneath the room floor like a giant insect.

"They had to have come in through the door," Harriet said as they piled back into the Road Hog and headed back to the security office. "It's the only option left."

"Right." Alex looked glum. "And that means that someone on the staff is lying. Either a staff member added the nicotine to the mask or a staff member let Sequoia or Leighton inside that spa room to do it. Either way I have to take a closer look at everyone who was working that day."

CHAPTER FIFTEEN

Alex and Fox dropped Harriet off at the business offices on their way to take Solly to his greenhouses. They were no closer to figuring out how someone had murdered Alice Haggedorn than they were the day she died and the morning had left a pall of dejection over them all.

Jeeves welcomed Harriet with his usual reserved yet pleasant greeting and reported no visitors, much to her relief. She wasn't sure she could face Sequoia and Leighton–or anyone else for that matter–with any semblance of equanimity this morning.

She pulled her dress heels from her knapsack before tossing it on a chair but didn't put them on. She'd found that she felt most comfortable working in bare feet. As long as her heels were readily available she didn't see why she couldn't go barefoot in the privacy of her office. She was in the islands after all, and the word formal was barely acknowledged.

After pouring herself an iced fruit drink Harriet headed for the lanai doors but veered off to wish her parents a good morn-ing. She contemplated their holo as she sipped the drink. They'd been a happy looking couple and obviously in love.

Why couldn't she remember more about them? She'd been what—seven or eight when they had died?

Other than one or two brief flashes of a very shadowy memory she had nothing. Shouldn't she remember *something* about those early years?

Had her mother sung to her? Had she taught her how to cook or garden or make flower leis? Had her father carried her on his shoulders or played ball with her or read to her? What had they been like as parents? Loving? Indifferent?

She bit at her bottom lip and tried to *feel*. She was convinced they had loved her, she realized, but she had no concrete memories to base that on. *Had* they loved her? Or was it just wishful dreaming on her part? Every child wanted to be loved, to feel special. Surely she had been no different.

The familiar migraine started throbbing in her skull but Harriet ignored it.

Her Aunt Wendolyn, her mother's sister, had told her nothing about their lives before the accident that claimed both her mother and her father. Harriet had asked about them often when she first went to live with her aunt and uncle, then she had abruptly stopped. Was that because she'd been given no answers?

Feeling frustrated by current events and her unknown past, Harriet finally gave in to the threatening migraine and took an analgesic. She needed to work, needed to focus on what she could do to help the resort. She needed to do her job. The Haggedorn murder would blow over once something more interesting caught the fickle attention of the news hounds.

What she really needed was to be ready with a new ad campaign that would wow the public and bring back guests.

Harriet opened the lanai doors to let in the sea breeze. She was happy to see the skim board family back on the beach. This time the daughter landed on her board when she leaped for it and stayed on for several long seconds before losing her balance. Harriet smiled at the young girl's shrieks of laughter.

The resort was a top notch destination for families, lovers, and individuals needing a break from the stress of their daily lives. She needed to remember that and focus on the good things the resort offered.

Her ad campaign featuring the amusement park had been a huge hit. The footage of guests riding the massive rollercoaster and the antique carousel that had been lovingly restored by Braxton Holliday, the amusement park manager, had brought in scads of queries and reservations.

Apparently riding the world's best roller coasters was a thing, a life goal–like climbing the world's over ten thousand foot mountain peaks, or surfing the world's best waves. Who knew? Harriet had included the footage in her ad because it added a level of excitement. And the carousel had added color and historic interest.

She'd since learned that the Island Resort Carousel had made number one on the list of best carousels in the world. The list was understandably short. The resort's carousel was the only fully restored and original carousel in the world.

She sat and swiveled her desk chair so she could look out the open doors while she thought. She needed an entirely different campaign. At some point she intended to do one on their Murder Mystery Dinner theatre, but this was not the time.

Maybe she should focus on the marina with its variety of sail and power boats, kayaks, jet skis, power tubing, parasailing, waterskiing, fishing . . . No, most island resorts offered some type of water recreation. While she fully intended to do a campaign centered around the marina at some point, right now she needed something with more of a wow factor.

And then she had it. She placed a quick call to Alex to let him know she was leaving her office and heading north. He insisted on sending Fox with her. Harriet tried to tell him that she'd be fine but she didn't argue too much. After her own near murder just a few weeks before she found that she still felt somewhat vulnerable. She liked Fox and welcomed his company.

Harriet grabbed her vid equipment, locked the lanai doors, and laced on her sneakers, then went out to the lobby to wait for Tarbell. The morning's disappointment was gone, replaced by the energizing rush she always experienced when she came up with a brilliant idea.

Tarbell didn't keep Harriet waiting long. He handed her into one of the resort's golf carts and they set off.

"So where are we going? Alex said north. I assume you aren't in a great hurry or I would have insisted that the boss give me the Road Hog." He looked at Harriet and smiled.

Tarbell had a nice smile with even white teeth. His smiles lit up his green eyes. Harriet thought that Tarbell Fox's natural inclination was to smile. Even so, she knew that like Alex, Tarbell had once been a cop and he thought like a cop. He had gotten a bum deal when he'd killed a junkie who was threatening his life.

Unfortunately the junkie had been related to someone important in politics and Tarbell had lost his job. He'd worked a series of menial jobs after that, drifting aimlessly until getting hired as a bellhop for the resort's hotel.

Alex had looked at Tarbell briefly as a suspect in the resort's last murder but quickly knocked him off his suspect list–and hired him away from the hotel, giving Tarbell a reason to smile again.

"Nope, no big hurry," she told him, returning the smile. "We're headed to Angel Brothers Circus. Have you checked it out yet?"

Tarbell's eyebrows rose. "The circus? Great! I haven't been there yet. They're set up a little farther north of the amusement park, aren't they?"

"Yes. North and a little more inland. I want to get some footage for a new ad campaign I'm thinking of creating so we'll get to see it all since I won't know what I need until I edit my recordings. I've heard they have old-fashioned food booths with fries and corndogs and popcorn and ice cones and the like so I thought we'd have lunch while we're there. I need to immerse myself in the whole experience to be sure I do them justice."

"I'm in. Sounds like a perfect way to spend a lovely afternoon."

They chatted comfortably for the remainder of the drive until Harriet spotted the circus tents' long, skinny, resort-blue banners flying above the treetops. "Take this right," she directed Tarbell.

The right fork was wide and smooth, with a brightly-colored sign picturing a circus tent and "Angel Brothers Circus" in decorative script. Harriet grabbed the vid camera from her knapsack and took a shot of the sign and the boldly striped tents with their blue banners flapping in the breeze while Tarbell pulled into the parking area.

"This looks like a real circus. I didn't know they still existed," Tarbell said as he waited for Harriet to climb out of the cart and join him.

"According to my research Angel Brothers is the only remaining full circus still in operation. They would only agree to work for the resort if they could have four months a year to do their annual European tour. As I understand it, Madame ZaZa is the direct descendent of the circus's founder. They've toured Europe for more than two hundred years."

"Unbelievable. It's hard to imagine anything lasting that long. Does Madame ZaZa play an active part in the circus?"

Harriet's eyes sparkled. "Oh, yes. She's the fortune teller-slash-tarot card reader. We will definitely be paying her a visit."

CHAPTER SIXTEEN

Even though all activities on the island were free to the resort guests, there was a gate at the entrance of the circus similar to the one for the amusement park. An attractive and very shapely young woman dressed in a glittering green skinsuit greeted them with a big smile.

Harriet watched Tarbell's eyes light up with appreciation and she was suddenly glad she'd let him accompany her. She had a suspicion that the young man's life had not been an easy or pleasant one since being kicked off the force. She made a silent vow to make sure he enjoyed his protection duty for the day even though he'd been ordered to come with her.

The young greeter—Tamara—gave Harriet directions to Madame ZaZa's tent but warned them that the fortune teller was in seclusion until her shift began.

"That's no problem," Harriet told her. She indicated the camera in her hand. "I have lots of things to shoot until Madame is ready to see me."

The next two hours passed swiftly. Harriet found far more to record than she had expected. Colorful stilt walkers towered over the guests. One bent down to tuck a red paper flower behind Harriet's ear.

"How did he do that?" she asked Tarbell after the stilt walker had moved on. "He should have fallen over. How did he keep his balance?"

"He's probably been practicing since he was a young boy. I wouldn't be surprised if most of the performers grew up in the circus. A family legacy thing, you know? Let's check out this tent."

Tarbell started to dart through the tent opening before remembering why he was there. "Sorry. After you," he said sheepishly.

Harriet laughed. "I'm glad you're enjoying yourself. I have to admit that it's all pretty wonderful."

They watched animal acts—Harriet loved the wild cats and the graceful horses. They watched men swallow swords and flaming sticks and shoot crossbows and knives at pretty women who never flinched even when they were spinning on a wheel. Harriet and Tarbell oohed and ahed along with the crowd and a few times she found herself gripping Tarbell's arm in alarm.

She had to remind herself more than once that she was there to record the action.

"Let's head over to Madame ZaZa's tent and see if she can squeeze us in before she gets busy." Harriet tossed her greasy fry wrapper in a convenient trash can. The fries had tasted wonderful doused with vinegar and salt. She'd have to tell Solly about using vinegar and salt on fries. She knew her friend would love them.

They passed a bright blue food tent that sold ice cream. Tarbell stopped and stared. "Now how is that even possible?" he asked Harriet, pointing to the sign. "It says 'fried ice cream.' You can't fry ice cream. It would melt." He shook his head. "The things they'd have you believe."

"I must say they do a great job of keeping this place clean," Tarbell remarked a few minutes later as they left the food court.

There wasn't a single piece of trash to be found on the ground. A crew of teens policed the circus grounds and kept them immaculate.

He tossed his own wrapper and grinned at Harriet. "Are you going to ask Madame ZaZa to tell your fortune?"

Harriet shook her head. "Nope. I don't believe that anyone can see the future. I want to let her know I'm here recording and that I plan to feature her circus in an ad campaign. What about you? Will you ask her to tell your future?"

"Nope. I agree with you. No one can tell the future. And even if she could I'm not sure I'd want to know. There's her tent."

They walked up to the small red and white striped tent. A double sided wooden sign identified it as Madame ZaZa's. The image on the sign depicted a woman with flowing black hair and an embroidered shawl holding a clear glass ball.

"Shall we?" Tarbell held the tent flap aside for Harriet.

The first thing Harriet noticed was the tent's dim interior. Lit only by three large candles that stood nearly chest high, the interior walls were draped in richly colored and patterned fabrics. The hustle and bustle of the circus seemed muted inside the small tent, as if the tent's canvas walls were somehow insulated against the outside noise.

Harriet walked over to the candles and pinched a flame between her thumb and forefinger. The flame went out and immediately popped back to life. Fake flames. She breathed a soft sigh of relief. Real candles would have been a fire hazard.

The second thing Harriet noticed when she turned around was Madame ZaZa herself.

The fortune teller resembled the image on the sign in that she had long, thick black hair and wore flowing garments and a colorful shawl. A shimmering gold turban topped her head.

Bangles and rings adorned her arms and fingers and enormous gold hoops hung from her ears.

What the sign image did not convey was Madame ZaZa's eyes. They were large and luminous and very, very dark. Harriet wondered if they were black. She had a difficult time looking away from them.

Madame ZaZa could have been any age from forty to eighty-five. She had a voluptuous build and she spoke in a deep, husky voice.

"I have been expecting you. You are Harriet Monroe?" she asked, indicating that Harriet should take the hard metal chair opposite her.

"I am. And this is Tarbell Fox." Harriet smiled and slid into the offered seat. Madame ZaZa inclined her head briefly toward Tarbell but never took her gaze off Harriet.

A small table covered with a heavily embroidered cloth separated them. On the table sat a deck of tarot cards and a clear, smooth round ball that appeared to be made of glass. Or was it crystal? Madame ZaZa's hands lay relaxed on either side of the ball.

"You have both been enjoying my circus?"

"We have. Your circus is absolutely wonderful, Madame ZaZa. Neither of us had ever experienced a circus before and I can honestly say, at least for me, that it is beyond anything I had imagined. I should be able to create several excellent ad campaigns from what I've recorded today."

Madame ZaZa's hands lifted to the crystal ball although she didn't touch it. She floated them up the ball's sides and over its surface in a mesmerizing pattern while her eyes never left Harriet's. She kept this up for a long minute before dropping her hands to the table and frowning.

"Give me your hands, please." Her bangles jangled lightly as she held out both of her own toward Harriet.

"Oh, no. You don't have to tell my fortune, Madame ZaZa. I

only stepped in here to introduce us to you and to compliment you on your circus."

Madame ZaZa said nothing. She continued to stare at Harriet and hold her hands out, obviously waiting for Harriet to do as asked.

Blushing, and feeling not a little foolish, Harriet placed her hands in Madame ZaZa's. She didn't know what she expected, but it wasn't the heat that seemed to flow from the fortune teller's hands into her own.

Madame ZaZa turned Harriet's left hand up and inspected it closely. "Despite what the sign outside this tent says, I do not read everyone's fortune," she said in that peculiar, husky voice. "It does not always reveal itself to me. With you however it is strong. When that happens I have no choice. I must follow my calling.

"Life has not been an easy ride for you thus far, my dear, but you are strong. You will be fine–eventually. But first there is a powerful barrier that you must overcome. It will not be easy, and at times it could even be physically painful. Indeed, it has already shown you pain."

The fortune teller stopped talking and pursed her lips. Her eyes blanked for a moment, as if the person within had gone away, before focusing again on Harriet.

"Yes. The barrier is strong and there is a great deal of pain involved with it. You must persevere if you wish to get to the truth. I can promise you that the pain will stop if you stay strong and see it through. All you question will be revealed."

Harriet's pulse began to race. Weren't fortune tellers supposed to tell women that they were going to meet someone tall, dark, and handsome or that they would win the lottery? Why would Madame ZaZa give her a fortune that sounded so awful? She suppressed a shiver and wished they hadn't visited the fortune teller.

"There is someone waiting to help you. You would be wise to accept that help."

Madame ZaZa released Harriet's hands before she could snatch them away. "As for the other, you have not found the correct answer yet. You must keep looking. That is all I have for you today. Please enjoy the remainder of your visit."

She stood and disappeared through an opening in the rear of the tent–majestic, dark, and mysterious–leaving a bewildered Harriet still sitting at the table.

CHAPTER SEVENTEEN

"Whoo! *That* was bizarre! Did you have any idea what Madame ZaZa was talking about?" Tarbell held the fortune telling tent flap open for Harriet. She stumbled through, still reeling from Madame ZaZa's words.

The bright sunlight felt blinding after the shadowed interior of the tent.

"It sounded pretty ominous." Tarbell looked curiously at Harriet. "All that talk about a barrier and pain and getting to the truth sounded like it came right out of a mystery or horror story."

Harriet took off her knapsack and slipped the vid camera inside with shaking hands. She couldn't look at Tarbell. Not quite yet. She pulled the knapsack back on and headed for the front gate, making her way blindly through the meandering guests while she took deep breaths to steady herself.

"*. . . there is a powerful barrier that you must overcome.*" What barrier? She tried to recall Madame ZaZa's exact words. "*The barrier is strong and there is a great deal of pain involved with it. You must persevere if you wish to get to the truth.*"

What truth? What sort of pain? And who was waiting to help her?

She had no idea what the fortune teller meant and she didn't want to think about it here with Tarbell and all these people. She needed to go home and walk the beach. Maybe seek out Solly. He was her only trusted friend. Was he the someone willing to help her?

He had to be. Who else was there?

Harriet shook her head. She didn't believe in fortune tellers, so why was she letting Madama Zaza's words get to her? She plowed into a couple walking arm in arm. Embarrassed, she apologized and slowed her pace. Tarbell gave her a funny look.

"You all right? You didn't let that charlatan rattle you, did you? It's just a game for the tourists."

Ignoring Tarbell's question, Harriet asked him what he thought Madame ZaZa meant when she said Harriet hadn't found the correct answer yet. She looked at her companion and frowned.

"Do you think maybe she meant that 'we' didn't have the correct answer yet? She did say we should keep looking."

Harriet stopped and grabbed Tarbell's arm. "Maybe she was referring to Alice Haggedorn's murder. That *has* to be it. Maybe Alice's granddaughter and her fiancé didn't kill her. Maybe it was someone else. We haven't considered that possibility."

Tarbell shot Harriet a sideways look. "Are you saying you believe what the fortune teller told you? I thought you said you didn't believe that a person could tell the future."

"I didn't. I don't. But she wasn't really telling the future, was she? She was basically saying we aren't looking in the right place. Maybe she heard something from one of her customers and is trying to help us."

"If she knows something then why hasn't she contacted Alex to share it with him? Leighton's plan to sue the resort and give it a bad rep affects everyone who works here. You'd think Madame ZaZa would try to stop that if she could."

"Maybe."

Harriet wasn't ready to give up on her theory yet. "And maybe she doesn't know about Terence Leighton and Sequoia Haggedorn and their plan to sue the resort for money."

They climbed into one of the many golf carts parked in the circus's small lot and headed back toward the main resort and business offices. Tarbell picked up the argument after they turned back onto the main road.

"It still comes down to you believing Madame ZaZa, Harriet. Did you in fact believe what she told you?"

Harriet looked away and watched the jungle growth pass by the cart. A brilliantly colored red and blue parrot squawked and flew across the road in front of them. The bird's bright black eyes seemed to scold them for disturbing its peace.

"Harriet?"

"I'm thinking. There was something there, Tarbell, something that felt like Madame ZaZa knew what she was talking about. What she had to say wasn't all fairy tale princes and happily ever after. It felt . . . honest, I guess."

She had expected Tarbell to snort with laughter, but he drove in silence. Several minutes passed before he spoke again.

"Okay, let's assume that Madame ZaZa knows what she's talking about. Who are the other possibilities for our murderer and why would they take an innocent woman's life?"

Thankful that Tarbell was focused on the murder and not the other message Madame ZaZa had given her, Harriet took a deep breath and focused on the new possibilities.

"First, maybe someone whom Alice Haggedorn had wronged in some way is here on the island. We didn't know Alice–maybe she was a bitch."

Tarbell raised his eyebrows. "Fine. Alice Haggedorn was a bitch. Is that a valid reason to murder someone?"

"Maybe she had an affair with another woman's husband or lover." Harriet twisted sideways in her seat to look at Tarbell. "I've read that poison is typically a woman's choice of murder weapon.

It could have been a revenge murder. That means Alex can eliminate the men on the island and concentrate on just the women."

"*Or* a man knows that poison is typically a woman's weapon and chose to use the nicotine to make the investigators think a woman did it."

Harriet's shoulders slumped. "Crap. It could be anyone."

Tarbell patted Harriet's knee. "It could be anyone and we don't even know if Madame ZaZa was talking about the murder. *And* there's the possibility that Madame ZaZa could be a complete charlatan and her words meant nothing."

Harriet straightened to look forward again. She didn't believe Madame ZaZa was a charlatan. She had felt an energetic connection between her and the mysterious fortune teller.

She had felt it when the older woman had gripped her hands and she had seen it in Madame ZaZa's darkly compelling eyes. She shivered at the memory of those eyes boring into her own.

They spent the remainder of the drive back to Harriet's office in silence, each lost in their own thoughts. Tarbell dropped her at the door and bid her a good day, then headed off to find Alex and tell him they needed to broaden their search for the murderer.

Harriet thanked him for accompanying her and headed inside. Jeeves greeted her without his customary smile.

"Ms. Montgomery has been looking for you," he said. "I am to ask you to go to her office as soon as you return. She seemed quite . . . upset. "

"Great." Harriet didn't want to deal with Cassie's problems right then. She had intended to lock up the vid camera and head immediately for home. The trip to the circus had drained her in more ways than one and left her feeling jumpy. She desperately wanted to be alone to think.

Unfortunately she couldn't ignore Cassie. The woman was not only a co-worker, she was fast becoming a friend. "I'll go see her right away, Jeeves. Thank you."

Harriet hurried down the office hallway without her usual delight in the large mural and knocked on Cassie's door.

"Cassie? It's me, Harriet."

The door slid open. Cassie stood on the other side. Her recently cut dark brown hair stood in tufts around her head. It looked as if Cassie had grabbed handfuls of her hair and tried to pull it out of her scalp.

"Bad day?" Harriet guessed.

"You could say that. Alex released the news that Alice Haggedorn was murdered and is refusing to let anyone leave the island until he clears them. I've been getting calls all day from irate business persons who are sure their offices will fall apart if they aren't allowed to leave immediately."

She glared and pointed a finger at Harriet. "You knew she was murdered, didn't you? Don't bother to deny it. You could have told me."

"I–"

"Forget it. Alex probably made you take a vow of silence. Lemonade?" Cassandra poured two glasses of lemonade without waiting for an answer and plopped onto one of her brightly patterned chairs. "Now what do we do?"

Harriet sighed and took the seat next to her friend. Cassie had every reason to expect her help. She was the public relations director after all.

"I'm not sure there is much we can do at the moment," she said carefully. "Guests can't leave until Alex is sure they aren't connected to Alice Haggedorn or her granddaughter in some way. The only thing you can tell them is that the sooner they cooperate with Alex the sooner they can get back to their offices. Maybe have the ones who need to leave right away give Alex their names so he can concentrate on clearing them to leave first."

"What a mess. Another murder. This place hasn't even been

open two months. Quit finding bodies, will you? This is all your fault."

When she saw the look on Harriet's face Cassie set down her lemonade. "Hey, I was only teasing. Of course this isn't your fault. I was trying to make a bad joke."

Cassie heaved a sigh and glared at the buzzing comm unit on her desk. "Pretty soon the media will be calling us Destination Death." She grinned then. "Hey, that one's pretty good, huh?"

Harriet smiled in spite of herself. "Yeah, that's pretty good," she agreed. "It fits right in with our Murder Mystery dinner theatre. I can see my next ad campaign." She raised her hands, framing an imaginary image and spoke in a low, portentous voice.

"Need to bump someone off? Come to Destination Death, the finest resort in the world, and rid your life of the one person standing in the way of fortune or love while you enjoy the finest amenities a resort can offer."

The two women grinned at each other. Harriet felt a little of the darkness that had enveloped her since her visit to Madame ZaZa leave her.

"I love my job," Cassie said. "I'm not going to let a murder or two ruin it for me and you shouldn't either. We'll get through this one like we did the last one."

The comm buzzed again and Cassie heaved her bulk from her chair. "Thanks for stopping by, Harry. I just needed to vent on someone. Let me know if there's anything I can do besides soothe angry Type A business persons. We're in this together."

Harriet returned to her own office, locked the vid camera away, let Alex know she was headed home, and left the office. Once she was walking alone on the shell road her strange meeting with Madame ZaZa came flooding back.

What truth? What barrier?

What had the fortune teller been trying to tell her? More to the point, why did it feel important?

CHAPTER EIGHTEEN

Venus Cottage next to Mermaid was empty, much to Harriet's disappointment. She stood on Solly's back lanai and stared out at the water. There was a bright band of turquoise near the shore sandwiched between the cobalt blue of deeper water and the white sand beach.

It struck her that the colors of the island seemed to come from a different spectrum than those of New England. Here they were brighter, richer, more . . . welcoming and alive. Could colors be alive?

Should she wait for Solly or take a run by herself? Alex was worried about her safety, and if she was absolutely honest with herself she did feel a little jittery and maybe even a teensy bit paranoid.

That damn fortune teller! Why had she even sat down at the table with her? And why, oh why had she let Madame ZaZa hold her hands? She could still feel the almost burning heat that had rushed into her hands from the Madame's. How had she done that?

Harriet paced the lanai, willing Solly to come home. She spotted some recent additions–brightly painted clay pots containing pungent green herbs. Solly must have brought them home for cooking, she mused. She ran a hand over the top of one, releasing its rich scent into the air. Rosemary.

She could call him at work but she didn't want to risk pulling him away from an important task. It wasn't that she felt that she was in danger in any way, she told herself. She just felt . . . out of sorts . . . confused.

Solly would drop everything for her if she called, just like she would for him. They were each other's family, the only family that mattered. She pulled her link from her shorts' pocket, then slipped it back in. She had been leaning on Solly too much lately.

The only person on the beach this far south was an older woman in a large floppy hat walking a tiny dog. Harriet hadn't known that pets were allowed on the island. The woman must have rented one of the separate cottages–the hotel would never allow pets because of people's allergies.

She filed the information away for possible inclusion in a future campaign. There were many people who refused to travel without their pets and insisted on pet friendly destinations. She made a mental note to check with Cassie and ask about the resort's official pet policy.

Thinking about work eased her frayed nerves. She kicked off her sandals and set them by the steps of Solly's lanai. She needed exercise. There was no reason for her not to take her run alone.

She walked down to the firmer damp sand before turning south toward the mangrove swamp. The guests rarely used the southernmost section of the beach, preferring instead to walk the central portion of the island closest to the hotel and restaurants.

Other than the length of pristine, deserted beach, there was nothing on the southern tip for the guests. The buildings on the southern end of the island were all utilitarian. Inland from the beach sat the laundry, situated next to a very long garage that stored the motor and sail boats, jet skis, kayaks, and other water toys that needed repairs, repainting, or storage. A mechanic's garage sat next to it.

Solly's seven greenhouses lived beyond those buildings. Harriet and Solly's cottages were two of the only four employee residences that sat on the beach. So far no one had moved into the two cottages that flanked them.

Harriet welcomed the sun's warmth through her tee shirt as she picked up her pace to a slow jog. Her bare feet sank slightly in the cool, damp sand with every stride. It didn't take long for her to feel the familiar burn in her calves that running on sand brought.

A seagull called overhead, its body impossibly white against the blue sky. She turned her head when something flashed in the water and was rewarded with the sight of a pod of dolphins curling back into a wave.

A group of small shorebirds on legs like stilts ran ahead of her, darting down to the water's edge to pluck unseen objects from the sand and racing out of the way of incoming waves.

The peace of the island seeped into her body and slowly worked its magic on her brain. She forced her thoughts to turn off, refusing to follow and get caught up in them, until all there was in her mind was the pounding of her feet and her labored breath.

She stopped running before she reached the mangrove swamp and walked slowly in circles while she waited for her heart rate to return to normal.

A sob escaped her throat. And then another. She wiped her cheeks with her hands, surprised to find them wet with tears.

Shocked by the unexpected rush of emotion, Harriet sank to her knees and covered her face with her hands. She struggled to rein it in, to regain control and tuck her feelings away as she had always done, but the flood gates were open–a great rising wave of pain so deep and all-engulfing she could barely breathe swept through her body.

She had no choice but to give in to it. She hugged herself as great gulping sobs filled with despair and hurt consumed her in a way she had never allowed before. Loud keening wails ripped from her throat and made her chest ache.

Why couldn't she remember anything about her mother and father? Surely there should be scraps of memory. All she had was this terrible empty space inside, this deep sense of abandonment.

The sharp searing pain of a migraine stabbed through her skull, toppling her onto her side in the wet sand. She curled herself into a tight ball and closed her eyes against the painful sunshine, willing the migraine away. She continued to cry until all that was left of her was an empty limp shell.

"Harriet? Jeezus, Harriet. *Sweetheart.*"

Masculine hands gently ran over her body.

"Is she–"

"Alive. Harriet, darling, what happened?"

Strong arms lifted her and pulled her close. She knew it was Alex and curled into his firm, warm chest. Cold. She felt so cold.

She heard the panic in his voice and wished she could tell him not to worry but she couldn't find the strength to speak. She couldn't even find the energy to open her eyes.

"Solly, go back for a cart. It will be faster then carrying her all the way back to the cottage. I'll meet you up on the road."

Harriet felt lips brush her temples and over her eyes. "Hang in there, sweetheart. I don't know what happened, but whatever it is we'll fix it. I promise. I'm here now. If anyone has hurt you they can't run far enough or fast enough to escape me. I promise you that too."

Minutes passed. Harriet heard Solly's voice again. Close, but at the same time far away. She felt Alex climb into the cart and settle her on his lap. He kept her pulled tight to his chest and she knew that he was trying to share his warmth with her. It surprised her to realize she was trembling.

"Can't this blasted thing go any faster?"

Harriet heard the humorous undertone in Solly's negative answer. She pressed against Alex's warmth and dozed.

"Hold her while I open the door."

She felt herself handed off and recognized that a different set of arms–not quite as strong–and a different chest–not quite as broad–held her. "Solly."

"Yes, babe. I've got you. You gave us both quite a scare you know. I think my heart actually stopped beating when we saw you lying on the beach."

Harriet felt a drop of moisture fall on her cheek and realized her friend was crying. "Don't cry," she whispered.

"Shhh. If I can't cry for you who can I cry for?"

They entered the cottage and Harriet felt Solly settle her on her bed. She still hadn't opened her eyes. Consciousness and awareness were both slowly coming back and with them a growing sense of embarrassment.

"I'm okay." Her throat felt raw and her chest ached. She *wasn't* okay, but she didn't want the men to know that.

"Of course you are," Solly soothed. "I'm going to draw you a hot bath. You're still shivering."

"Already on it."

Harriet felt the bed sink beside her and knew that Alex had joined them. His hand smoothed loose strands of hair away from her face. Her eyes felt swollen and she knew her face had to be blotchy from her weep fest.

Unwanted tears leaked from her still closed eyes. It felt so good to be fussed over and taken care of.

She had been doing for herself for as long as she could remember. Her Aunt Wendy had not been an affectionate woman, and while she had done her duty by Harriet after the death of Harriet's parents, she had made no effort to become a second mother to the orphaned young girl. There had been no signs of affection, no "I love you" after the loss of her parents.

Solly squeezed her hand. She hadn't realized that he held it. "I'll be right back," he said. He returned a moment later. "Tub's ready."

Despite her protests, several minutes later Harriet found herself stripped down to her underwear and sitting in the slipper tub amid a massive mound of aromatic bubbles. The hot water seeped into her body and began to thaw the core of ice that she identified as what had once been the center of her being.

Could someone's soul freeze? If it was possible then that was what had happened to her today.

The doors next to the tub had been opened, letting in the warm evening air and the scent of the night-blooming flowers. She let her head relax against the back of the tub and rolled it to the right to observe the two men sitting on the floor, watching her closely. An unexpected laugh bubbled from her chest.

"I'm okay," she croaked. "I won't drown in the tub, I promise."

Solly stood and handed her an iced glass of fruit juice. "Drink. You're dehydrated."

Harriet took the glass and sipped. The sweet-tart juice laced with rum tasted wonderful and the cold soothed her throat. She downed the drink and handed the empty glass back. "More."

"Yes, madame, your command is mine to obey." He grinned at her, the relief plain in his warm brown eyes, and left to refill her glass.

"Harriet." Alex waited for her to look at him before continuing. "I don't know if you heard me earlier. Whatever it is, we'll fix it. I promise. You aren't alone."

Harriet's throat closed up. She felt the pressure of fresh tears pushing at her eyeballs. She couldn't speak so she settled for a nod and sank lower into the bubbles.

She drank a second glass of juice and finally looked alert enough that the men agreed to leave her to finish her bath and dress. While she dried herself she could hear them talking in low voices out in her living room. They would want an explanation. Of course they would. So would she if their roles were reversed. And they deserved one.

But what could she tell them? That a fortune teller had spooked her and precipitated a total meltdown? She didn't really know what had happened other than she had completely lost control of herself.

Harriet sighed and pulled on the clean sweatpants and long sleeve tee that Solly had dug out and left for her. She didn't have the energy to deal with her thick hair so she left it hanging loose.

It was time to face the music.

CHAPTER NINETEEN

Alex and Solly stopped talking as soon as Harriet walked into her living room.

"You look a little more human at least," Solly teased her. "You scared the bejeezus out of me, Harry. Don't ever do that again. I found your sandals on my lanai and no sign of you. I called Alex right away and we followed your tracks down the beach. Don't ever, ever scare me like that again," he repeated.

Alex said nothing. Harriet was uncomfortably aware of his close scrutiny. "I'm fine," she said, doing her best to glare at him. "You don't have to watch me like you're afraid I'm going to collapse."

"And she's back," said Solly. "Tell us what happened, Harry, and don't even think of leaving anything out. I'll know. What happened at the circus today? And what happened on the beach?"

Harriet sank onto the couch and tucked her legs up beneath her. She studied the two men sitting opposite morosely. She had to tell them about the visit to Madame ZaZa. The chances were good that Tarbell Fox had already told Alex about it and Alex had shared with Solly.

This is what happened when you let people into your life–you had to share pieces of yourself with them.

"I stopped by Madame ZaZa's fortune telling tent with Tarbell today." Her voice sounded low and ragged. "She took my hands and when she did it was like liquid fire flowed from her hands into mine. I hadn't expected that."

She repeated what Madame ZaZa had told her nearly word for word, then sat back and closed her eyes. They snapped open when she felt a nudge on the shoulder. Alex held a bottle of water toward her.

"Drink this. You need more fluids."

She took the water, drank it down, and still felt thirsty. She must have used up all of her body's moisture crying. How humiliating.

"Okay," Solly said. "Let's start with the first thing the good Madame talked about. A barrier, pain, and truth. Did that mean anything to you?"

Harriet felt so grateful that her friend was taking her seriously that she almost started crying again. She choked back the tears and took a deep breath. She was not a crybaby. Never had been and wasn't going to start now.

"No." She started to shake her head but that hurt so she stopped. "I couldn't think of anything. Maybe Madame Zaza was referring to something in my future."

Solly frowned. "All right, we'll set that one aside for now. What else did she say?" He snapped his fingers. "Right. 'You haven't found the right answer and must keep looking'–or something to that effect. What do you think she was talking about?"

"Alice Haggedorn's murder." Harriet replied without hesitation. "It's the only thing that fits. And if we don't have the right answer yet then Sequoia and her blue haired beau are innocent."

Alex groaned and wiped a hand down his face. "Unfortunately I'm inclined to agree with Madame ZaZa. I've tried–lord knows

I've tried–and I can't come up with anything that tells me Sequoia and her beau did the murder. For one thing, as you've pointed out before neither of them seems particularly bright. Whoever found a way to add nicotine to that body mask was intelligent. I still haven't been able to figure out how it was done."

"What about the way Terence Leighton and Sequoia jumped on the opportunity to sue the resort and Douglas Wade?" Harriet asked. "That was smart."

"Agreed. Smart and something only a lawyer would think of. And that's exactly what happened. A lawyer overheard Sequoia and Leighton talking about her grandmother's death and made a few 'suggestions' to them to make some easy cash."

"I heard you've publicized the fact that Alice was murdered."

Alex shrugged one shoulder. "There was no reason to keep it quiet any longer. I'm hoping that by making it public knowledge someone will come forward with new information."

They sat in silence for several minutes, until Harriet felt a hand on her shoulder. She jerked her head up and realized that she had fallen asleep. "Sorry. I guess I'm a little worn out."

Solly stood and headed for the lanai doors. "I'm going to make some dinner. Should I bring you both a plate? Or would you like to come over when it's ready?"

Harriet shook her head. "I'm not hungry, Sol. I just want to go to bed."

"I'll pass too, but thanks for the offer."

Harriet saw some silent message pass between them. Solly hesitated a moment, then nodded and left.

Alex placed an arm around her and helped her to her feet.

"I'm fine," she protested, detesting the weakness of her voice.

"Sure you are, but I'm not. I swear I lost ten years from my life when I saw you lying on the beach. I'm going to tuck you into bed and then I'm going to stay with you until you fall asleep."

"You don't have to." Harriet swallowed. "But I'd be grateful if you did."

Alex swept her up and deposited her in the center of the king-size bed, pulled a lightweight blanket over her, then lay down beside her and wrapped his arm about her waist. Harriet snuggled back against him, grateful for his warmth and the feeling of security his presence brought her.

When she woke from dozing Alex still held her.

A half moon was shining through the open lanai doors. She could hear the soft rush of the waves lapping the beach and the chirp of crickets. She heaved a big sigh. Everything in her life felt like such a confused mess.

Alex's arm left her waist. She felt his hand gently move her hair aside and the soft touch of his warm lips moving over the back of her neck. A shiver of excitement shot through her body.

Her ex had never held her like this. Bradley had never displayed tenderness toward her, or made her feel wanted or attractive. Somehow Alex managed to do all three with his gentle touch.

What had she ever seen in Bradley Higgins? she wondered. She'd been such a fool. Solly had tried to warn her about Bradley but she hadn't listened. She'd been so caught up in having a *boyfriend*, and then a *fiancé*, that she hadn't been able to see beyond her dream of belonging to someone.

The dream of being precious to one special person.

Harriet rolled over to face Alex and lifted her mouth to his. He kissed her slowly, gently. As if he had all the time in the world and meant to savor every moment of it. Harriet's arm crept around his waist and she pressed against him, reveling in his strength and pure masculinity.

They broke off the kiss and looked at each other in the semi-dark. Alex reached up to brush her hair back from her face and cupped her cheek, rubbing his thumb over her cheekbone.

"Not tonight, Harriet. Lord knows I want you, but I want more than just sex with you. I want the whole enchilada. I need your love and I want your trust."

Harriet almost told him that she loved him right then, but bit back the words. How did she know whether or not she loved Alex? She *thought* she did, but then she had thought herself madly in love with Bradley Higgins and she couldn't have been more wrong. More important, Alex hadn't said that he loved her.

"I trust you," she said.

Alex kissed her temple. "If you trusted me you'd tell me about your parents." He knew he was pushing her, but damn he wanted her to trust him.

No, he amended, he *needed* her to trust him. As long as Harriet kept the truth about her parents from him there could be nothing more between them. He wouldn't settle for a marriage built on half truths.

The thought gave him pause. Yes, he had meant it, he realized. He really did want the whole enchilada. He wanted to marry Harriet Monroe and raise a family with her.

"My parents?" Bewildered, Harriet pulled back and frowned at Alex. "Tell you *what* about my parents? They died in an accident when I was eight." The familiar dull throb of an impending migraine began to beat in her skull. Damn migraines.

Alex's hand dropped to her waist, imprisoning her. "Fine. We'll start there. What kind of an accident? How did they die?"

The dull throb in Harriet's head beat harder and faster. "I don't know," she whispered. "My aunt would only tell me they died in an accident. I don't *know* any more than that."

Alex's eyes became hooded. "You were there. You must remember."

"I was there?" Her voice rose. "How do you know–" The migraine escalated to a searing pain that stabbed and clawed at her like a ferocious beast trying to devour her brain. Sparkles of light flashed in front of her eyes.

"I can't talk," she gasped. She grabbed at her temples and rolled away from him. "I can't talk," she repeated.

Alex stilled behind her. She expected him to leave, but after a long minute his arm came around her waist again and he pulled her against him.

"We'll talk about this in the morning," he said. "Go to sleep."

CHAPTER TWENTY

Alex pushed his hand through his hair as he stood in the middle of Harriet's living room. He felt frustrated by Harriet's refusal to come clean about her parents and clueless as to what to do about it. Unable to sleep himself, he had left her once he was sure she was sleeping peacefully and come out here to pace and think.

Why couldn't she talk with him about her parents? How long would she keep up this lie about not remembering? She had been there when they died. The truth was bad, but what happened hadn't been her fault.

Maybe he should just tell her that he already knew the truth. That he knew she'd been the only survivor of a cult's mass suicide.

He paced to the bedroom door and back and stopped in the middle of the room again.

Was it possible that she truly didn't remember?

He plopped onto a chair and leaned his forearms on his thighs. He had read of cases where a person experienced something so traumatic that their brain walled it off and refused to let them access it. Could that have happened to Harriet? What she had witnessed would leave scars on anyone, no matter their age or how strong they were.

He turned his head and looked at the doorway leading into Harriet's bedroom.

If Harriet was telling him the truth and she really couldn't remember how her parents had died then he was behaving like a dick. What right did he have to push her into telling him about an event that had turned her entire life upside down? Forcing her to remember something her brain could be trying to protect her from was irresponsible and harsh.

The big question was, was it possible that she had suppressed the memory?It made sense now that he thought about it. What could be more traumatic for a young girl than to watch her parents–and her friends and essentially everyone she knew–commit suicide?

Jeezus. Was he the kind of man who turned his back on someone he loved when they most needed help? If it was better for Harriet to forget then he was being a prick trying to force her to tell him about the day her parents died.

Alex leaped to his feet and started for the bedroom. He needed to be there when she woke up and apologize for being so insensitive. He needed to be the support he'd promised Harriet he would be.

When he entered the bedroom he saw Harriet's shape huddled in the middle of the bed and heard her whimpering and gasping in pain.

"Ah, geez, sweetheart, I'm so sorry." He lay on the bed and gathered her stiff body as close as he could.

"I was th-there?" Harriet could barely squeeze the words out between her chattering teeth. Her head pounded. Lightening bolts pinged inside her skull. "You s-said I was there."

"I'm sorry," he crooned, stroking her back. "I was stupid. Forget I said anything. Shhhh. We don't have to talk about this. I'm sorry I brought it up."

"No!" Harriet pushed away from him. "I n-need to know. T-tell me. What happened to my parents?"

"Fine. Okay. To start, your name is Twinkle Monroe."

"Twink–ahhhh." Harriet grabbed at her skull and huffed through the breathing technique she had learned to help mitigate the headache pain. Unfortunately it never got rid of the pain completely, only lessened it. This time it had no beneficial effect at all.

Alex waited until her breathing had slowed before he spoke again. "Your parents changed their names to Starlight and Arcturus when they joined a cult. When you came along they kept with the star theme and named you Twinkle. When you went to live with your Aunt Wendolyn she had your name legally changed to Harriet."

"Twink–" The pain in Harriet's skull expanded until she thought her skull would explode.

Alex held Harriet and rubbed her back with long, smooth strokes, waiting for her to regain consciousness. While he waited he examined what had happened.

Harriet had not been faking her pain. He had heard it in her voice, seen it in her beautiful eyes, and felt the tension in her body as she fought to deal with it. Ultimately it had proven to be too much for her to handle and her brain had shut down.

Fortunately her breathing had smoothed out and her body lay relaxed against his now.

There was something seriously wrong with Harriet's situation. Something he didn't understand. He was afraid to tell her any more about her parents until he knew more about Harriet's affliction, and Aunt Wendolyn was the only one alive who could answer his questions.

Unfortunately he had to wait until he could get back to his

office to call Harriet's aunt. He didn't want Harriet to overhear whatever Wendolyn had to say about the situation. Would the aunt even tell him—a complete stranger—the truth?

What a mess. His heart bled for the little girl named Twinkle who had lost her parents, and for the young woman named Harriet who couldn't remember them without suffering debilitating pain. How much psychological damage had been done, and was it even possible to undo it? Had her aunt ever sought professional help for Harriet?

He bent his neck and saw that Harriet was awake again and watching him warily. He gave her a wry smile and kissed her mouth. "Go to sleep," he said softly. "We both need to go to work in a few hours."

Harriet closed her eyes and was asleep within seconds.

Alex however, spent the night watching the moon dip into the ocean and wondered how he was going to set Harriet's world right.

When Harriet opened her eyes again the pale pink light of an island dawn filled her bedroom. She felt physically wrung out the same way she had after once trying to run a marathon she hadn't trained well enough for.

Bradley had been disappointed by her poor showing, she remembered. Today she would tell him to go jump off a pier. Back then she'd felt only shame that she'd let him down.

She stretched her arms and froze when she felt the large body next to her. Memories of the previous day came flooding back and she stifled a groan. She'd made a right fool of herself letting Madame ZaZa get to her. She had frightened both Solly and Alex. So much so that they'd watched her take a bath and Alex had slept with her. They hadn't dared to leave her alone.

Well, Alex had sort of slept with her, she amended. She was

under the blanket while he lay on top of the blanket, so did that count as sleeping together?

"Good morning."

Startled from her rambling thoughts Harriet rolled over to face her . . . what? What was Alex to her? More than a friend, less than a lover. She settled on special friend with potential.

"Good morning," she answered with a smile. "You didn't have to guard me all night, you know. I was fine after my bath." She saw surprise flash in Alex's eyes and disappear just as quickly.

"Couldn't take the chance," he said, pulling aside the gauzy insect curtains and rolling out of the bed with the fluid grace that reminded her of a large cat. "Solly wouldn't leave until I promised to keep my eye on you."

"Ah-ha! Was that the silent between-us-men message I saw you two signal each other?" she teased. She exited the opposite side of the bed. "I have first dibs on the shower, then I'll make coffee." Grabbing a clean work outfit she disappeared through the door, still smiling.

Alex watched her go. Whatever he had expected to face this morning it wasn't the cheerful, carefree Harriet that had appeared. What the devil was going on?

He thought back to the emotional scenes of the previous night and ran his hand through his hair and massaged the back of his neck. Whatever Harriet had experienced when he mentioned her given name and her parents had been real. The pain in her head had been real.

So why the happy face this morning? Did she really not remember last night? Could that be another symptom, or aspect—or whatever he should call it—of her problem?

Harriet's behavior almost mirrored someone who was bipolar. Up, down, happy, sad, energized, lethargic. Except that whatever was wrong, it wasn't that simple.

He needed help. Whatever was going on in Harriet's brain

was beyond his experience. He needed to speak with the aunt as soon as possible.

CHAPTER TWENTY-ONE

The entire resort was buzzing with the news that one of the guests had been murdered. Alex walked into the security office after seeing Harriet to her office door and paused. Every chair along the outer wall was taken. A group of three stood at the refreshment bar chatting. Two more guests were at the counter questioning Mary.

"Good morning," Alex said quietly. More than a dozen pairs of eyes swiveled toward him. The seated guests stood and rushed toward him but stopped when Alex held up his hand.

"I don't know why you are all here, but I assume it has something to do with Alice Haggedorn's murder. I just walked through the door so forgive me if I take a few minutes to organize myself. If you'll please give your name to Mary I'll set up an interview room and speak with each of you individually."

He let himself into his office and grabbed a notepad and his personal PC. No time to contact Harriet's Aunt Wendolyn this morning. It frustrated him to have to wait, but the resort guests came before personal matters.

He called Fox and asked his assistant to meet him in the interview room next to Fox's own office, then locked up and headed across the lobby to the opposite hall.

"Mary, do you have that list of names?"

"Yes, Mr. Hayes." Mary handed him a printout.

Alex looked at the number of names in surprise and frowned. "There are a lot of names on here."

"Yes, Mr. Hayes. You've had a number of calls this morning as well. I separated the people who are here in person from the callers." She indicated the second column of names on the sheet.

"That's very helpful. Thank you, Mary. Well, let's get started." He looked at the gathered guests and called out the first name on the list. "Mr. Robberts? Will you come with me, please."

A portly man with a balding head and fleshy lips pushed forward. "I'm here. I have important information for you regarding Mrs. Haggedorn's murder." He looked around at the others waiting and puffed out his chest.

"Right this way, Mr. Robberts." Alex clamped down on his irritation and ushered the pompous little man to the interview room, offering him a refreshment from the room's small juice and coffee bar. Once he had Mr. Robberts settled Alex sat next to Fox.

"All right, Mr. Robberts, what would you like to tell us?"

Mr. Robberts leaned forward, his unexpectedly attractive hazel eyes gleaming. "I talked with Alice Haggedorn once, you know, before she was killed. She was seated at the table next to me in the hotel's dining room, waiting for her granddaughter to join her. Pretty little thing, that granddaughter." He winked at Fox.

Alex suppressed a groan. The odds that a guest had real, useful information were slim but he had to go through the motions in case one of them really did know something.

"And what did Mrs. Haggedorn have to say that you believe could help us find her murderer?"

"Well." Mr. Robberts sat back and hooked his arm over the

chair back in an effort to look nonchalant. "Alice–Mrs. Hagge-dorn–told me that her granddaughter's boyfriend had shown up at the resort even though it was supposed to be a vacation just for Alice and her granddaughter." He gave his head a curt nod as if he had just shared an earth-shattering piece of information.

"All right. And?"

A look of surprise came over Mr. Robberts' face. "What do you mean 'and'? Don't you see?" He leaned forward and jabbed the table with a pudgy finger. "The boyfriend did it. He came here specifically to bump the old lady off. Mark my words. He knew Alice Haggedorn didn't like him." He sat back again and crossed his arms over his chest in a self-satisfied manner.

"All right, Mr. Robberts. Thank you for coming in. You've been very helpful. Mr. Fox will escort you back to the lobby." He handed the list of names to Fox. "Bring back the next guest, will you please?"

"God save me from arrogant busybodies," he muttered after Fox had escorted Mr. Robberts from the interview room. He had a feeling it was going to be a long morning. Unfortunately he had no choice but to hear what each and every guest who had called or arrived in person had to say about Alice Haggedorn.

Still, Mr. Robberts *had* told them something new–Sequoia's boyfriend had not been invited along.

Three long hours passed so slowly that Alex wanted to cross his eyes and bang his head on the table. The list of names grew longer as more guests heard interviews were being conducted. They showed up at the security office to "do their duty" for poor, murdered Alice Haggedorn. Most had nothing more to offer than the fact that they had seen Alice with the granddaughter or the granddaughter's boyfriend.

It was early afternoon before Alex was able to have Fox escort the last guest from the interview room. He sat back and closed his eyes while he waited for Fox to return.

The long night and lack of sleep were dragging on him. In his previous life as a NYC murder detective he'd put in many a double shift and had gone without sleep for days when he was hot on the trail of a killer.

But that was then, and one of the reasons he'd gotten out of the murder game. The other reason he'd quit the force was that he'd become fed up with dealing with scumbags every day.

Who would have guessed that taking the job as head of security on a fancy island resort would have him hunting down murderers again? He knew he shouldn't complain. At least the scumbags on the resort were a higher class and dressed better.

"You look beat." Fox slid into the chair opposite Alex. "That was a lot of hours spent listening to self-important jerks who came here mostly to hear themselves talk. Oxymorons."

"Did you just call our esteemed guests oxymorons?" Alex couldn't help himself, he grinned at his assistant.

Fox grinned back. "No, but if the name fits . . . I was referring to their way of relaying facts that were nothing more than gossip. True gossip is an oxymoron. Unconfirmed tales that they wanted us to buy as truths." He shook his head. "Did we get anything useful out of them?"

"Two things." Alex pushed back his chair and stood. "First, it seems that Alice Haggedorn did not care for our blue haired fiancé Terence Leighton."

"And second?"

"Second, I announced the murder yesterday afternoon. Why haven't we heard from Sequoia Haggedorn and her beau? They should have been beating down the security office door demanding to know more."

Fox raised an eyebrow as red as his hair. "You're right, boss. Are we going to pay them a visit next?"

"Not next. Let me have that list of names." Alex took the list and neatly tore it, handing one piece back to Fox. "First we finish speaking with any guests who claim to know something about the murder. You call those names, find out what they have to say.

I'll call my share. We'll compare notes and *then* we'll pay Miss Haggedorn a visit."

Two hours later Alex shut down his link and stared at his bare office walls. Only one of the guests he'd spoken with had anything even slightly interesting to add to the morning's interviews. He buzzed Fox to meet him out front. It was time to have a conversation with the granddaughter.

CHAPTER TWENTY-TWO

Harriet spent the morning in her office editing the vid footage she had taken the previous day at the circus. She ordered lunch in and instructed Jeeves not to put through any calls. Editing was a slow, focused process that called for a great deal of precision and concentration.

Since she enjoyed detail work, she enjoyed editing as much and maybe more, than she liked the filming. Editing was where the real act of creation took place, where she put together something that was uniquely her own. Editing was where she reached out to people and touched them—nudged them—to take a specific action. In this case her goal was to make others aware of what the resort had to offer.

How many destinations boasted a real circus *and* an amusement park with the world's only original wooden carousel? How many offered the best in water sports, a top-notch spa, five star accommodations and food prepared by some of the world's best chefs?

Only one: The Island Resort.

Cassie stopped by briefly to inform Harriet that—as they had expected—several guests had called to cancel their reservations and even more were trying to make bookings for a stay at "Destination Death".

"They aren't really calling the resort that, are they?" Harriet asked in horror.

"Nah. I just like the sound of it." Cassie grinned. "I've decided not to let any of this get to me. Alex will do his job and this too shall pass. I found it interesting that the first murder brought out the ghouls, which I admit was a big surprise to me. This one is confirming that there are a lot of sick bastards out there."

Harriet gave her new friend a weak smile in return. "As long as Mr. Wade doesn't shut down the resort I don't care who our guests are. Wait. I didn't mean that. I'd hate to have a bunch of real murderers show up here."

Cassie laughed and left, leaving Harriet sitting at her desk unable to refocus on her new ad campaign. She stared into space, her mind working the problem of how the murderer was able to sneak the nicotine into the body mask. Wasn't the *how* the whole key to finding out who?

She drummed her fingers on her desk but knew she wouldn't get back to the editing until she took another look at the spa. Mind made up, she left a message with Mary to let Alex know where she was going and headed out.

She had no trouble finding a free resort cart. The guests left them everywhere and just grabbed any one they found when they needed to go somewhere. It was a system that seemed to be working well.

The sun was shining, the air comfortably warm and not too humid. The greenery and colorful flowers, birds, and other wildlife entertained Harriet on the trip north to the spa. She especially loved the lizards, having never seen a real lizard before coming to the island. Their leathery skin and marble-like eyes that moved independently of each other made the creatures look prehistoric and enigmatic as they stalked the ground and foliage for their next meal.

The heavy scent of the Angel's Trumpets hit her as soon as she parked in front of the long, low, spa building. She took a minute to walk over and inspect the enormous, trumpet-shaped flowers. They were truly spectacular. The pale green throats of the blooms measured nearly a foot long, with their trumpets opening wide in delicate shades of yellow and peach. Small insects crawled inside the blooms.

How large were the bats who fertilized the massive flowers?

She hated bats. One had gotten stuck in her hair once when she and Solly were searching dumpsters near Portland's waterfront for useful items to sell. She had been unable to do anything but shriek and dance around until Solly could untangle the bat from her hair.

Harriet shuddered at the memory and scurried to let herself into the spa. The place was definitely back in business. Soft music played from hidden speakers blended with the fall of water into the koi and lily pond. Fat, white, waist high candles burned on either side of the black granite reception desk.

Raylene looked up, smiled and welcomed her.

"Miss Monroe. What can we do for you? I'm afraid all of our treatment rooms are booked." The pretty receptionist looked honestly regretful.

Harriet returned the smile and offered her carefully prepared semi-lie. "I'm not here for a treatment today, Raylene. I wondered–if Alice Haggedorn's room is still off limits would you mind if I took a look at it? Alex knows I'm here."

It was mostly the truth. Maybe not the whole truth, but basically the truth if she discounted the possibility that Alex may not have received her message yet. She smiled at Raylene and hoped neither she nor Aaron thought to call Alex and ask his permission.

Raylene, who had looked uncertain, brightened when Harriet mentioned Alex. "If Alex knows you're here then I don't see any reason why not," she said with another smile. "Just let us know when you leave, okay?"

"Of course."

Harriet walked slowly until she was hidden by the waterfall wall, then quickened her steps. What was she doing there? She didn't have a clue, and now that she was at the spa her decision to visit the murder scene felt impetuous and foolish. Still, she was there, so she may as well check it out.

She let herself into the room where someone had figured out a clever way to take the life of Alice Haggedorn and stood just inside the door. The room needed a cleaning. Leaves had blown in through the open wall and dust covered every surface.

She could still smell the lemony, herbaceous scent of the essential oil the masseuse had used on Alice Haggedorn before applying the deadly mask.

Harriet set her knapsack on the floor by the door and walked over to the granite counter that held the hot rock heater, the oils, and the body mask heater. The insert containing the remainder of the murderer's mask had been taken away for testing. She opened and smelled a few of the massage oils before turning to the table in the center of the room.

Okay. What were the sequence of events? Alice Haggedorn had entered the room, undressed, and donned a spa robe. Her masseuse had joined her a few minutes after that. The masseuse would most likely have had the mask heating so it would be ready when she finished Alice's massage.

Pretending she was Alice, Harriet scooted onto the massage table and lay face down, positioning her face in the cutout in the table. With her face firmly in the hole Harriet could see neither to the right nor the left. Alice would have had the same restricted vision.

She sat up and swung her legs off the table and stared at the palm tree Solly had climbed.

No one could have snuck into the room unless they came

through the door pretending to drop off towels or some other item while Alice lay on the table. They had proved that the day Solly climbed the palm tree.

Harriet frowned. How had the person known that Alice was lying on the table and therefore unable to see who came in?

She walked to the door and let herself out, closing the door behind her. Standing in the hall, it was clear the heavy paper that filled the Japanese-style door blocked any view of the treatment room interior.

She slid the door open a couple inches but couldn't see the massage table even with her eye pressed against the opening. She kept sliding until the table came into view. Six inches, a gap wide enough that Alice would definitely have noticed if she had still been standing.

That was too great a risk for the murderer, Harriet decided. She reentered the room and stared at the table, trying to reason out the sequence of events.

There were only three possibilities: someone had spiked the body mask with the poison before Alice arrived for her appointment. (Most likely)

The masseuse had poisoned the body mask. (Unlikely)

Or . . . Harriet shook her head. The third option made no sense at all.

She turned and headed for her knapsack just as the door slid open. Alex walked in and closed it behind him.

"Solve the mystery yet?" he asked. His smile didn't quite knock the weariness from his eyes.

Harriet felt her cheeks warm. This was the man who had spent the night in her bed. On *top* of the blanket, but still. They had *slept* together.

"No." She cleared her throat. "I was trying to reconstruct what happened. I was hoping it might give me some ideas."

Alex took a step closer. "Interesting. And a useful technique I've often used myself. Did you come up with anything?"

"Nothing useful, I'm afraid. What are you doing here?"

"Mary gave me your message. I thought I'd see what you were up to. Plus it gave me an excuse not to interview any more 'helpful' guests."

Harriet studied his face, saw the fatigue there and realized it was because of her. "I'm sorry you were involved in my meltdown yesterday. I don't know why, but for some reason Madame ZaZa got to me. Thank you for hanging in there and staying with me. It was kind of you."

Alex crossed the distance between them in three long strides and cupped Harriet's face between his strong hands. "It had nothing to do with kindness, Harriet. I care about you. A lot. I don't know what's going on in that brain of yours but I'm going to help you figure it out."

Harriet felt a flush of embarrassment. Why was he making a big deal of her meltdown? Wasn't a girl entitled to lose it now and then?

A light tap sounded on the door before she could defend herself. A dark face surrounded by blonde curls appeared in the opening.

"Mr. Hayes? I knew I saw you come in here." A woman came into the room without waiting for an invitation.

Alex stepped away from Harriet and gestured toward the woman. "Harriet, this is Nakeesha Bain, Alice Haggedorn's preferred masseuse. Nakeesha, this is Harriet Monroe, the resort's PR director."

Harriet looked at Nakeesha curiously. She appeared to be in her early forties, although enhancements could easily erase ten years or more from a face. She had a compact but shapely build and a no nonsense demeanor.

I'm pleased to meet you, Ms. Bain," she said, smiling. "I was just trying to reconstruct Harriet's last visit to the spa. Can you tell me if you turned on the mask heater before her arrival? I assumed you'd want it warmed and ready as soon as you finished her massage."

Nakeesha nodded. "Tha's right. My massage puts 'em to sleep, you see. I don't like my people to get too asleep and then have to wake up for me to mud 'em so I do the mud right away. Then they can nap without bein' disturbed."

"I've heard that Mrs. Haggedorn always asked for you. You must be very good at what you do."

Strong white teeth flashed in Nakeesha's dark face. It was obvious that Harriet's comment had pleased the masseuse. "Sometimes I can see a person needs a little extra pamperin'. Mrs. H was one a those people."

"What makes you say that?" Harriet asked. Alex shifted slightly beside her and she knew he was listening closely. "Did Alice seem stressed or worried about something?"

Nakeesha wagged her head slightly side to side, making her curls bounce. "Not worried bad, but not really happy, you know? Her Sequoia got herself hooked up with a man Mrs. H didn't like much. She fretted 'bout the situation some when I had her on the table. I tol' her to let it go. Jus' let it go, I say to her." She shrugged a shoulder.

"Did you need me for something, Nakeesha?" Alex asked.

"No sir. Jus' wanted to know when I can have my room back, tha's all."

"I don't think it can tell me anything more than it already has. You can go ahead and book it."

Nakeesha smiled again and disappeared.

"Ready to go?" Alex gestured Harriet out the door ahead of him.

Neither of them spoke on the way out to the parking pad.

Alex stopped beside Harriet's cart and waited for her to strap in. "Don't head home alone." He leaned down and kissed her cheek. "I'll be at the cottage in time to cook dinner."

Feeling slightly bemused by the knowledge that Alex planned

to cook her dinner, Harriet drove back to her office with Alex on her flank the whole way. When he saw her head inside he honked his horn and peeled off.

Once inside her office Harriet made no attempt at even pretending to work.

Alice Haggedorn's masseuse had told them that Alice had been upset over Sequoia taking up with Terence Leighton. That was information they hadn't known before. What, if anything, did it mean?

CHAPTER TWENTY-THREE

Alex tagged Fox on the link after following Harriet to her office.

"It's time to bring Terence Leighton and Sequoia Haggedorn in for a talk. Let's see what they have to say for themselves. See if you can track down Sequoia. I want to talk with her first. Bring her to the interview room and tag me when you get there."

Alex checked in with Mary before heading into his office. She gave him one more name to contact, a housekeeper who thought she might have some useful information. He thanked her and checked his watch, calculating. With any luck he had time to contact Harriet's Aunt Wendolyn and see if she could shed any light on Harriet's migraines and her inability to remember her early years before Fox arrived with Sequoia.

The woman who answered the link looked nothing like the warm, attractive woman in the holo Harriet kept in her office. If it wasn't for the fact that the aunt had Harriet's nose minus the bump he would not have guessed they were related. The aunt's dull gray hair was scraped back from her face and pinned into a tight knot, her expression stiff and disapproving and decidedly unattractive. Wendolyn Wainwright looked cold and unapproachable.

Alex plowed ahead anyway.

"Mrs. Wainwright? My name is Alex Hayes. I'm the security director for The Island Resort. I wondered if I could ask you a few questions about your niece."

"I have nothing to do with my niece." The woman's expression grew colder if possible. "If she's in trouble that's *her* problem," she added in a dry, rasping voice. There was a glint of satisfaction in her eyes that put Alex's back up.

"You misunderstand, Mrs. Wainwright. Harriet isn't in any kind of trouble."

Harriet's aunt sniffed. "Then why are you calling me, Mr.–what did you say your name is?"

Alex was beginning to regret placing this particular call after a day that had already stretched his patience thin.

"Hayes. Alex Hayes. I'm calling because I think Harriet might need some help and–"

Wendolyn Wainwright didn't give him time to finish. "We gave Harriet all the help we could after my sister died. The ungrateful girl tried to make trouble and ran away in thanks. She's an adult now. We owe her nothing."

"Could you tell me if your sister Starlight–"

"My sister's name was Belinda, Mr. Hayes, not *Starlight*." Alex could practically see disdain drip from Wendolyn Wainwright's mouth as she spoke the name. What a thoroughly unpleasant woman. Life with her must have been a cold hell for Harriet.

"Starlight was an affectation my sister's worthless husband talked her into. I don't appreciate you calling me out of the blue and bringing up such an unpleasant subject. Good–"

Alex knew she was about to cut him off. "Mrs. Wainwright, Harriet is suffering from intense migraines and periods of amnesia. Is there a history of either of those in your family?"

For several long moments he didn't think she was going to answer, then he saw her chest rise.

"What makes–"

"*Wendy!* Who are you talking to?" The image on Alex's link spun and centered on a red-faced man with two hefty chins, bushy gray eyebrows, and a large fleshy nose. "Who are *you*?" he demanded.

"He's a security director," Alex heard Wendolyn Wainwright answer in the background. "He's asking about Harriet."

Anger flashed in the man's flat brown eyes. "Whatever trouble that twit of a girl is in now has nothing to do with us. We disowned her as soon as she made those ridiculous accusations about me and good riddance to her."

Alex had a pretty good idea what those accusations were. Poor Harriet. His temper, already on a short fuse, flared.

"*Mr.* Wainwright, put your wife back on the link. *Now.* Or I'll make sure those accusations are made public. I'm sure your neighbors would be very interested in hearing what kind of a pervert they live next to."

He would do no such thing of course because it would hurt Harriet, but Arthur Wainwright didn't know that.

Wainwright sputtered and harrumphed. His face grew redder and the image on the link spun again. Wendolyn Wainwright reappeared. Her already pale face looked even whiter. Two bright red spots dotted her cheeks.

Good. Alex had no patience for men who abused children in their care. And he had no sympathy for Harriet's aunt since she hadn't protected a child who had needed protecting, especially one under her roof.

"Mrs. Wainwright, I asked you a question. Do I need to repeat it?"

He watched Wendolyn Wainwright's eyes cut to the left. Was she waiting for her husband to move out of ear shot or debating if she should answer?

"I *will* come to Maine and ask my questions in person if you don't answer me now," he added in his softest, most menacing tone. "And I'll be only too happy to knock on your neighbors' doors and question them as well."

"I don't see how you have any right to pry into Harriet's personal problems."

Wendolyn Wainwright sniffed again. She might be rattled but she was holding firm.

"Harriet needs help. You can talk to me now or you can talk with me tomorrow in person. Your choice. But if I have to take the time away from my job to fly to Maine I won't be happy, and I'll probably tell your neighbors more than you'd like while I'm there." He waited a beat to see if she understood.

"Threats aren't necessary, Mr. Hayes. There are things from Harriet's early years that are better left forgotten."

"I'm listening."

"After her parents' . . . *accident* . . . we took her to a specialist. He programmed her to forget them."

Alex blinked. "Programmed Harriet? To forget her parents? How? What do you mean 'programmed her'?"

Wendolyn Wainwright had regained her cool, superior air. "It's a simple procedure, Mr. Hayes. A combination of aversion therapy and hypnotic suggestion. Whenever Harriet tries to remember her parents she gets what she probably thinks is a migraine. The harder she tries to remember the more severe the pain."

"That's barbaric. Why would you do such a thing to a child?"

The aunt's expression hardened. "No, it isn't barbaric at all. The technique is used all the time on soldiers who witness the atrocities of war that they can't live with once they return to civilian life. Harriet's doctor went a step further and set up a trigger that induces amnesia if she fights the pain block. As far as Harriet is concerned her life started at age eight. It's for the best. Leave well enough alone, Mr. Hayes."

Wendolyn Wainwright abruptly ended the call.

Alex stared at the blank link screen in disbelief. Could Harriet's aunt really believe that robbing Harriet of her memories and replacing them with painful headaches and amnesia was better for Harriet?

He didn't even know how to process that attitude. Nor did he know how to help Harriet. He suspected he would need to find another "specialist" who was familiar with the techniques used by the first specialist to remove the block.

His link buzzed and he clicked it on. Fox and Sequoia were waiting for him in the interview room. Harriet would have to wait.

It was time to switch gears and concentrate on finding Alice Haggedorn's murderer.

CHAPTER TWENTY-FOUR

Harriet felt confined and antsy. She had given up on the plan to get more work done after returning from the spa but Alex didn't want her going back to the cottage alone.

She paced her office, then sat at her desk and forced herself to work, but after messing up an edit she shut down her PC and paced her office some more, until she knew she would go batty if she didn't get out and move. She needed a run, or at the very least a walk on the beach.

She crossed to the lanai doors and checked the beach below the offices. There were at least a dozen people there, walking, sunning, snorkeling, and enjoying the beach outside her office. Surely she would be safe if she went out to join them.

Mind made up, she opened the lanai doors and stepped outside, grateful that she'd worn a pair of dress shorts with a sleeveless silk blouse to work. There was a light breeze blowing on shore, a breeze that would have made walking in a dress or skirt difficult.

She pulled the doors closed behind her and heard them lock. She wasn't worried about locking herself out of her office. Jeeves would let her in when she returned. The nice thing about using droids on the reception desk was that they were on duty twenty-four/seven.

The softer, deeper sand above the tide line felt warm and slightly abrasive on her bare feet as she headed to the firmer packed sand closer to the water. A middle-aged couple walking hand in hand nodded hello. Harriet smiled and felt herself relax a little. Apparently not everyone was bothered by recent events on the island.

She continued down to the water's edge and waded in to ankle depth. Slipping her hands into her pockets she stared out at the sunlit turquoise water and thought about her theories regarding Alice Haggedorn's murder.

Alice had not liked Terence Leighton. They had heard that from more than one source so she assumed it was a fact. Was it that Alice didn't care for him as a person? Or did she not like him because Sequoia was attracted to him? Had she disapproved of any other of Sequoia's boyfriends?

And how had Terence Leighton felt about Alice Haggedorn? Had he tried to win her approval, and when he failed had he resented her enough to kill her?

Sequoia had agreed to marry him. Had Alice known that before she died? Or was the engagement more recent? It would be interesting to know when the engagement had taken place. She'd have to remember to ask Alex when she saw him tonight.

The knowledge that she would be seeing Alex so soon gave her a little thrill. She could easily get used to seeing him before and after work. If only he hadn't witnessed her meltdown the previous day. It was humiliating to know he'd seen her at her very worst—with all her defenses down. She couldn't ever remember losing it quite like that before.

"Harry? I thought that was you."

Harriet turned her head. Terence Leighton was hurrying toward her. For a brief second she felt the urge to run, but a quick look around told her they weren't alone so she stood her ground. Surely Terence wasn't foolish enough to try anything in front of witnesses.

"Mr. Leighton. What can I do for you?" She slipped her hands from her pockets in case she had to defend herself or run.

Leighton stopped just shy of the water. He was wearing leather boat shoes along with another snug tee shirt advertising Terry's Gym, and snug running shorts covered his bulging thighs. Three sets of dangling silver balls hung from his left ear completed his outfit. Harriet noticed brown hair growing at the root ends of his electric blue locks. He had opted for violet contacts today.

He also looked tired and grim, his mouth curved down in an unhappy expression.

"You heard that Sequoia's grandmother was murdered?" he asked.

"Yes." Harriet had no intention of encouraging conversation with Leighton until she knew what he wanted from her. His next words surprised her.

"Alice Haggedorn didn't like me much. Can't say as I blame her." He took a deep breath, expanding his impressive chest, and let it out. "I pretty much screwed up my business you see. She must have known I was a bad risk for her granddaughter."

He waved a hand at the graphic on his tee shirt. "I own a gym. Or rather, I *did* own a gym. By the time I get back to New York the bank will own it. I'm sure Mrs. Haggedorn thought I was using Sequoia to get her money."

He looked at Harriet, his eyes pleading. "I wasn't though. I really love Sequoia. I know it looks bad but I knew Sequoia didn't have any money of her own–when we got engaged the old lady made a point of telling me about the trust she'd set up for Sequoia and warned me that I couldn't break it. I was hoping that if I showed up here I could make the old lady–I mean Alice– accept me. That's all I wanted."

Harriet looked at him, considering his words and weighing their sincerity. "How long have you been engaged?"

"About three months. Sequoia doesn't know I'm losing the gym yet. I didn't know how to tell her. She likes to brag about me." His voice sounded bleak. "I don't want her to think I'm a loser, you know?"

Part of Harriet felt some sympathy for Leighton. The bigger part remembered how he had invited the news media to the island and threatened to sue Mr. Wade.

"You talked Sequoia into suing the resort and Mr. Wade."

Leighton flushed. "Yeah, about that. I saw a quick way to save my gym. It's all I have, the only thing to show for all the years I worked creating this." He waved a hand down his body.

"I know you probably think I'm nothing more than a dumb jock but I had a dream. I moved too fast and tried to expand too big and I lost it all. If I had listened to my ex-partner I'd still have a business. I don't know what I'll do now. Body sculpting is the only thing I'm good at."

It was hard to stay angry with a not very bright jock who saw himself as realistically as Leighton did. Harriet felt herself soften toward the man.

"I love Sequoia," he repeated. "I want to marry her if she'll still have me. I'm just sorry that it's too late to make a good impression on her grandmother."

The tide had crept in while they stood talking. Harriet looked down and realized that Leighton's shoes were wet. He hadn't even noticed. That more than anything else convinced her that Leighton was sincere.

"Do you know who would want Alice Haggedorn dead?" she asked.

Leighton shook his head. "No. Sequoia loved her Gamma. Alice raised her after Sequoia's father OD'd and her mother ran off. I respected the old broad for that reason alone. She had bucks. She could have dumped Sequoia in a boarding school, or even denied the family ties and put her in an orphanage, but Alice took Sequoia in and raised her like a daughter. She loved her and gave her a good home."

A wave crashed and foamed around them. Leighton realized he was standing in water and made a disgusted sound but didn't move.

"I want to see whoever took my girl's grandmother away from her punished," he said, fisting his hands at his sides. "Gamma was all the family she had left."

Harriet reached out and touched him briefly on the arm. "She still has you," she said quietly.

Leighton grimaced. "Maybe. Maybe not, once she hears I've lost my gym." He turned and walked away, his shoes squelching in the hard pack sand.

Harriet watched him leave. Everything Leighton had told her held the ring of truth in it. She felt ninety-eight percent sure Terence Leighton was not the killer. And if Sequoia loved her grandmother as much as he claimed she did then she was not the killer either.

She stood thinking, staring blindly at the ocean until another wave splashed her knees. Having made a decision, she turned and hurried back to the office. Maybe there was something she could do to help Sequoia and Leighton move on with their lives.

CHAPTER TWENTY-FIVE

Alex sat alone in the interview room. Fox had escorted Sequoia from the building and was rounding up Terence Leighton to bring him in next.

He lowered his forehead onto his hands and rubbed his tired eyes. He hated cases like this, cases where there were legitimate suspects but no way to wrap them up. Sequoia had seemed honestly upset when he'd told her the cause of her grandmother's death. He didn't believe her shock was feigned.

He also didn't believe that Sequoia had killed her grandmother.

He had poked and prodded her about her lifestyle and her grandmother's money. The young woman seemed honestly happy with her lot in life and not at all bothered that she had to depend on a group of trustees for her money.

"Gamma has always been generous toward me. I have everything I need," she'd told them guilelessly.

Then Alex had poked and prodded her about Terence Leighton until Sequoia sat up straight in her chair and began to pay close attention.

"You think Terry had something to do with Gamma's death?"

she had asked, eyes wide. "Why would he want to kill my grandmother?"

"Perhaps he needed money," Fox had answered, trying to bait her. Both men had watched her closely. Alex had only seen confusion in her face.

"Why would Terry need money? He owns a gym. He's a successful businessman," she'd explained, her pride in Terry clear.

Alex had let Fox break the news to Sequoia that her fiancé was about to lose his business and owed a large amount of debt to several investors.

She had sat there in shock as the news sunk in.

Alex had felt like a heel. He told himself that Leighton should have been honest with Sequoia about the financial ruin he was about to face, but he still felt like a heel. He'd broken off the interview at that point and sent Fox after Leighton.

A brief knock interrupted his thoughts. Fox poked his head into the interview room. "I can't find Leighton. He isn't in his room or in either gym. Should we send out an APB on him?"

Fox grinned at his little joke. Since he and Alex were both ex-cops an "all points bulletin, or a 'be on the lookout" would have been the next step in their previous careers.

"Nah. Don't bother." Alex stood and tucked the chair under the table. "I've talked to enough people today. I need a break. Let's call it a day and start fresh tomorrow at oh-eight-hundred. Leighton isn't going anywhere."

"Fine by me, boss. There's a cute waitress just started working in the employee restaurant. I'm going to see if she'd like to have a drink with me later."

Alex waved his assistant off and headed back to his own office to shut down for the night. He looked forward to seeing Harriet, looked forward to sharing a bottle of wine and dinner.

Dinner. He groaned. He had told Harriet that he would cook dinner for her tonight. He needed to swing by the employee kitchen and see if he could sweet talk one of the chefs out of some fresh shrimp and garlic. He had a hankering for scampi.

It took another hour before he was able to swing by Harriet's office to escort her home.

"Ms. Monroe left forty-six minutes ago, Mr. Hayes," Jeeves told him. "She said she had something to check out."

Alex's blood pressure rose. Hadn't he told Harriet to stay put until he or Solly arrived to take her back to her cottage? He whipped out his link and called her, fuming.

"Where the hell are you?" he demanded. "You're supposed to be here."

"Hello, Alex. Where is 'here'?"

"Here. At your office. I'm here to take you home. I have dinner." He knew he sounded like a petulant teenaged boy but he couldn't seem to help himself. He was exhausted and annoyed.

"Where the hell are you?" he repeated.

"Talking to the housekeepers. I had a theory about Alice Haggedorn's death. I wanted to see if it holds water."

Alex made an effort to rein in his temper. "Can we talk about this at home?"

Harriet didn't say anything for a long moment. Did Alex realize what he'd just said? She searched his tired, irritated image. No. Calling Mermaid Cottage home had been nothing more than a slip of the tongue.

"Wait there," she said. "Give me ten more minutes. I'm almost finished here." She cut the link before he could refuse.

Alex stared at his blank screen. She'd cut him off? Didn't she realize he was there for her safety? He certainly wasn't pacing her office lobby holding a package of shrimp after a long, grueling day that had followed an even longer, *more* grueling night for his own pleasure. No sir.

He noticed Jeeves watching him and stopped his pacing. What was wrong with him? He never let things get to him like this.

He needed sleep. Dinner, wine, and a good night's sleep.

Unfortunately he wasn't going to get it on Harriet's living room floor. And he couldn't invite himself into her bed again. Last night had been unusual circumstances.

He sat in one of the lobby's cushioned seats and forced himself to relax. Leaning back and stretching out his legs, he crossed his arms over his chest and closed his eyes.

"How long has he been asleep?" Harriet had returned to her office building and discovered Alex lightly snoring in the lobby.

"Exactly eight minutes."

One thing about droids, Harriet observed, they were precise.

She watched the gentle rise and fall of Alex's chest. She hated to disturb him but he'd end up stiff and achy if she let him sleep. And lord knew the poor man needed sleep.

She watched him for a few more minutes before lightly squeezing his shoulder. His eyes opened immediately.

"About time you got here," he grumbled.

Harriet decided to let that go. "I'm sorry I kept you waiting. It might be worth it though once you hear what I've learned. Shall we go?"

Alex frowned at her and she knew he wanted to lecture her about leaving the office without protection, but he refrained. She gave him points for that even though she knew he'd probably scold her later when they were alone.

He surged gracefully to his feet and picked up a white paper-wrapped package from the seat next to him. "Let's go. I'm famished."

Harriet scooted into the golf cart's driver seat before Alex could take control. "I'll drive."

Alex didn't argue, just slid into the passenger seat and crossed his arms over his chest again. He fell asleep before she had even pulled away from the office.

CHAPTER TWENTY-SIX

Solly ended up cooking the shrimp scampi. Alex insisted that Solly join them for dinner when Solly popped in to check on Harriet, but when Alex fell asleep again after a pre-dinner glass of wine Solly took over the meal, much to Harriet's relief.

"I really need to learn how to cook a few more dishes," she told her friend while she watched Solly sauté the garlic and shrimp. Her kitchen smelled wonderful. "That dish looks easy enough."

"It is. And delicious. We'll make it again in a week or so and I'll guide you through the steps. The keys are not to burn the garlic and not to overcook the shrimp." Solly drained the pasta and dumped it in with the shrimp and aromatics.

"Alex seems pretty beat. He doesn't strike me as a man who usually falls asleep while he's waiting to eat." He waited a beat, then gave Harriet a sly look. "Tell me you finally hooked up with him."

Harriet flushed. "He stayed awake watching over me last night. I wish he hadn't taken my meltdown so seriously. I was fine after a good night's sleep."

"He cares about you, Harry. I was worried too, you know. I've never seen you so . . . gutted."

Harriet ran a finger over the smooth granite island while she struggled to come up with an explanation for what had happened on the beach. When she looked back up at her friend she wore a troubled expression.

"I don't know what happened to me yesterday, Solly. I've never broken down like that before. It was a little scary, to be honest. Once I started I couldn't stop."

"Do you think it had anything to do with Madame ZaZa's . . . uh, 'prophecy'? The bit about truth and pain?"

"I don't know. I was taking a run to clear away some of the stress from the day and realized I had tears running down my face. The next thing I knew Alex was lifting me off the sand."

Solly took the pan off the heat and gave it a last shake. "Speaking of Alex, go wake your boyfriend. Dinner's ready. We'll talk more later."

"He's not my boyfriend."

Solly raised his eyebrows at her. "You can't be that stupid, Harry. Hell, I *know* you're not that stupid. Alex is definitely sweet on you. Would he stay awake all night watching over you if he wasn't? No. And you're crazy about him. Take my advice and don't fight it. He's the best thing that's ever happened to you—next to me, of course."

Harriet couldn't help herself. She laughed. "I love you."

"I know you do, kid. Now go get Alex before this gets cold."

They had barely finished the meal when Alex's eyes began to droop again. Harriet quietly shooed Solly out of the cottage and returned to the table.

"Alex." She placed her hand on his shoulder.

Alex's eyes jerked open. "What?" he rubbed his hands over his face. "Jeezus, I fell asleep at the table, didn't I? I'm not as young as I used to be. Hard to pull an all-nighter."

"Alex, go to bed. I'll clean up here."

"Thanks." Alex grabbed his sleeping bag from the entry closet and wrapped it around him.

"Not there." Harriet had followed him into the living room. She took his hand and tugged gently toward the bedroom. "The bed is plenty large enough for both of us. You need a good night's sleep. You can't spend the night on the floor."

Alex knew he should refuse but he felt too drained to argue. He pulled his link from his pocket and set it on the bedside table, then lay on top of the bed with his sleeping bag wrapped around him and immediately fell into a deep sleep.

Harriet stood in the bedroom doorway and waited until she heard him snoring lightly before she went back to the kitchen. It felt good and right having Alex sleeping in her bed.

Maybe she should listen to Solly and not fight it. It was time to stop being afraid. She'd only been involved in one romantic relationship–a whopping failure–but that didn't mean this would be too.

She found herself humming as she cleaned up from dinner and got ready for bed. Fifteen minutes later she was under the covers and sound asleep.

Harriet opened her eyes and wondered what had woken her. She tensed, listening for an intruder but heard nothing except the gentle lap of waves on the beach and the dry rattle of palm fronds.

Something buzzed on the bedside table. Alex's link.

She rolled over and realized Alex was still deeply asleep and hadn't heard his link buzz. He'd thrown off the sleeping bag and lay on his back, his tee-shirt covered chest rising and falling rhythmically. He'd been too tired to bother to undress for bed.

Maybe she could grab the link and tell whoever was calling to call back in the morning.

Slipping out of bed so as not to disturb Alex, she tiptoed around the bed, grabbed the link, and took it into the living room.

"Block video," she commanded. "This is Alex's link."

Silence.

"Hello? This is Alex's link. If this is a crank call so help me I'll–"

"Harry? Is that you?"

Oh. How embarrassing. Harriet was glad she'd thought to block video.

"Tarbell. Yes. Alex is sleeping in the other room." No need to explain to Alex's assistant that the other room was her bedroom. Let Tarbell think Alex was in the living room.

"Why do you have Alex's link?"

So much for her clever ploy. Before she could answer Alex appeared in the doorway. Her heart gave a lurch. He looked so damn good, with his dark hair disheveled from sleep and the dark shadow of a beard on his face. She felt her pulse beating in her throat and swallowed.

"Who is it?"

"Harry? Where's Alex?"

Both men spoke at once. Harriet held the link toward Alex. "It's Tarbell."

Alex held out his hand and Harriet dropped the link into it. "Fox. What's up? *What?* I'll be right there."

He shoved the link into his pocket and headed for the door. "I have to go to the spa. Sequoia Haggedorn is threatening to kill Leighton."

"I'm coming too. I can help."

"Hurry up then and toss some clothes on."

It was only then that Harriet realized she wore only a thin tank and her silk underpants. Fortunately she hadn't turned on the living room lights. She squeezed by Alex and hurried to dress.

They took a golf cart to the security office and exchanged it for Alex's motorcycle. The Triumph roared to life, it's engine shattering the peaceful night. Harriet climbed on behind Alex and wrapped her arms tight around him.

She had hoped for another ride on the motorcycle, but not what followed. Alex raced the bike up the shell road to the spa, laying the bike so low on the curves that Harriet wondered if her calves would touch the road. It was both exhilarating and frightening.

Once, a large lizard appeared in the road in front of them, it's long body and tail taking up most of the width of the road. Alex cursed, downshifted, and guided the bike along the road's rough edge. The back end slid off the road and she heard Alex curse.

A branch stung as it caught Harriet in the upper arm. She tucked her head against Alex's back to protect her face. Then they were back on the road and roaring back to full power.

Ten minutes after receiving the call, Alex pulled up to the spa's front door. The heavy perfume of the Angel's Trumpet blanketed the parking pad. Harriet glanced over at the plants growing in the center of the circular drive and realized the massive pale trumpets were faintly glowing.

Just as she was thinking what a wondrous sight it was a large bat glided in and hung off a blossom.

Harriet shuddered and hurried after Alex's retreating form, eager to get away from any bats.

"Where are they?" she whispered, once they were inside. The waterfall wall had small blue-tinted spotlights shining up at it. The unlit spa lobby looked much larger without Aaron and Raylene and sunlight. She could see beams of moonlight piercing the jungle growth beyond the missing wall.

Alex didn't answer. A bad guy would be smart to beware of Alex Hayes in this mood, Harriet realized. He had to still be exhausted, running on only the couple hours of sleep he had snatched at her cottage, but he was fully alert–all business, all focused power. She had never met a man who could thrill her the way Alex did.

And this was definitely not the time to be thinking about that. She followed him behind the waterfall wall and down the hallway. They stopped outside the room where Alice Haggedorn had taken her last treatment.

At first Harriet heard only silence and she was afraid they were too late. Then she heard Fox's voice.

"Sequoia. This isn't the way to handle this. Do you want to spend the rest of your life locked in a cage? Let the law deal with Leighton."

"Wait here." Alex slid open the shoji door and stepped inside the room. "What's going on in here?" he asked, his voice friendly.

It didn't take long for him to assess the situation. Leighton stood on the edge of the floor with a thirty foot drop off only inches away. Sequoia held a police issue stunner on him. (And where had she picked up a restricted stunner?)

From where he stood Alex could see that she had the stunner set to full power. Even a brief shot would kill a man. Fox stood just inside the shoji door and to the right. He had his hand on his own weapon but hadn't drawn it yet.

"Hello, Sequoia," Alex said quietly. "What's going on here?" The couple were dressed for a night out, most likely at the resort's dance club.

Leighton wore tight black leather pants and a loose white shirt unbuttoned to his waist. Sequoia wore a body hugging red dress that ended mid-thigh with a diamond-shaped cut out that revealed her ruby-studded navel.

Sequoia gestured with the stunner, her mouth set in a grim line. "Terry killed my Gamma. You said so this afternoon. I can't let him get away with that. I loved my Gamma."

"I never said that your fiancé killed your grandmother. You misunderstood."

"Who else then?" demanded Sequoia. "There's no one else. It had to be Terry." Tears ran down her cheeks and the stunner trembled in her hand.

"I thought you loved me, you bastard. But you were just using me to get to Gamma's money. You've lost your gym and needed money and you used me."

Leighton's hand were in the air. He looked miserable and frightened. "I swear I didn't kill your grandmother, honey. I wouldn't take away your only family."

"Liar!"

Alex sensed movement behind him. Harriet stepped in front of him. He reached out to push her behind him, out of harm's way, but she evaded him.

"Sequoia. Listen to me. Terry is telling the truth," Harriet said quietly. "He didn't kill your grandmother. But I know who did."

Sequoia's head swiveled toward Harriet. So did Fox's and Alex's. Hope flared in Leighton's eyes.

"Who? Who killed my Gamma? *Tell me.*"

Harriet held out her hand. She had never seen a real stunner before but she'd seen pictures and knew what it was. She also knew that they had the potential to not just stun, but also to kill. She took a deep breath to slow her racing heart.

"Not until you give me the weapon. Someone could get hurt or killed and you would have to live with that for the rest of your life. Please, give me the stunner."

"You're lying. You're trying to trick me."

"No. I'm telling you the truth. I figured it out late this afternoon. I know who killed your grandmother and I'd be thrilled to tell you the whole story. But you have to hand over the stunner first. It wasn't Terry, I promise you that. He really does love you, Sequoia. His only crime was that he wasn't as honest with you about his gym as he should have been. And I suspect that's because he was afraid of losing you."

Sequoia was openly crying now. Tears colored with mascara left black streaks running down her cheeks. "Tell me."

"Give me the stunner." It took so long for Sequoia to respond that Harriet thought she'd lost her gamble. Then Sequoia crumpled to the floor and dropped the stunner.

"I miss my Gamma," she wailed.

Harriet hurried over to Sequoia and wrapped her arms around her. "Of course you do," she soothed. "Let's go somewhere comfortable where we can talk. All of us," she added, when she saw the naked pain in Leighton's eyes. How would it feel to have the person you love threaten your life?

She hoped the couple would be able to salvage their relationship but that decision wasn't hers.

CHAPTER TWENTY-SEVEN

They ended up at the resort's all night restaurant located on the roof of the two story hotel.

Harriet appreciated that the resort's developer had opted to keep all of the buildings unobtrusive, including the hotel. Mr. Wade could have chosen to build a monstrosity of a building that soared into the sky and housed a thousand or more guests, but he had opted to emphasize the exclusiveness of the resort instead and limit the number of guests who could be on the island at any one time to the hundreds rather than the thousands.

The open-air restaurant occupied the entire roof of the south wing of the hotel. A four foot high clear acrylic wall topped with a brass rail offered protection from falls and an unobstructed view of the ocean to the west and the jungle to the east. The thatched roof was supported by carved bamboo poles nearly a foot in diameter.

Because the building only stood two stories high, trees and vines covered with brilliant blossoms surrounded the diners, creating the impression that they were dining in a tree house.

Harriet led the group to a table in the far corner of the quiet restaurant. Laughter from a table of four women floated across the night air. Candles glowed softly inside pale blue blown glass holders. Moonlight striped the water and she could see the running lights on a ship far off to the west.

On another occasion the restaurant could be quite romantic, she reflected. She filed the knowledge away to include in a future ad campaign.

"You know who killed Alice Haggedorn?" Alex said quietly into her ear as he pulled out a chair for her. "And you didn't tell me?"

"I didn't have the chance," Harriet whispered back. "You practically slept through dinner." She ignored his scowl and turned her attention to Sequoia.

"Sit beside me, Sequoia," she said, patting the chair back next her. Sequoia had ceased shedding tears but her face still bore the dark streaks of her eye make-up. Harriet watched Leighton begin to take the chair next to Sequoia but move to the opposite side of the table when she glared at him.

She waited until everyone had settled and ordered drinks before she spoke. This wasn't how she had expected it to play out so she wasn't quite sure how to say what she had to say. If only she'd told Alex what she'd learned earlier when she had the chance. Then he could explain her theory to everyone and she wouldn't be in the hot seat.

Everyone looked at her. Fox's expression was curious, Alex's mildly irritated. Leighton looked like a man who'd lost a treasure and Sequoia's face expressed her distrust.

Harriet took a deep breath and let it out. She'd just have to wing it, she decided.

"The one thing that's been a stumbling block in solving your grandmother's death is how the nicotine got into her body mask," she began.

"Somebody put it there." Sequoia glared at Leighton.

"Yes, Sequoia. Somebody put it there. I could only come up with three possibilities. The first, that someone who worked at the spa put the nicotine in the mask before your grandmother arrived for her session. Alex looked into everyone who could have done that and was satisfied that it wasn't a spa employee."

"How can he be sure?"

"You can trust Alex to do his job, Sequoia. He was a highly respected murder detective before he came here to work for the resort and he knows what he's doing. You should consider yourself very fortunate that he's here."

The waiter arrived with their drinks and Harriet drank hers half down right away. Her mouth felt dry and her hands were shaking a little. The pineapple and soda water she had ordered tasted wonderful–cold and sweet and tart–and helped smooth out her nerves.

Harriet knew that not a single person at the table was going to believe what she had to say. She could feel Alex's eyes on her but didn't dare look at him. She kept her focus on Sequoia instead and pushed on.

"The second option was that someone snuck into the room from the outside to poison the body mask. Alex, Fox, my friend Solly–"

"Is that the really good looking man Terry and I saw you with when we came to talk to you?"

"Uh, yes. That was Solomon Ayers. I call him Solly."

"He's pretty dreamy."

Amused, Harriet agreed. "Yes, I guess he is."

"Can we keep this conversation on track here?" Alex did not sound amused.

Harriet didn't blame him. The poor man was still woefully short on sleep. She hurried on.

"Right. We tried every way we could think of to enter Alice's treatment room without leaving any sign that we had done so. It was impossible. Even with the open wall it is impossible to enter any of the treatment rooms by any method other than the shoji doors without making a great deal of noise or leaving marks on the wing walls that extend out beyond the floor."

Now came the hard to believe part. Harriet took another sip of her drink to fortify herself. When she looked up, everyone was leaning forward, staring at her, waiting to hear what she had to say.

"There's an old quote about eliminating the impossible . . . " She frowned, trying to remember.

"I know that one," Fox said. "It's a quote from a famous fictional detective named Sherlock Holmes from several centuries ago. He said that once you eliminate the impossible, whatever remains, no matter how improbable, must be the truth."

"Exactly!" Harriet beamed at him. "Once we eliminated all other sources of the nicotine, it left only one."

"Son of a bitch," Alex said softly. "Alice Haggedorn poisoned herself."

Harriet looked at Sequoia and gently took the girl's hand. "Alex is right. Your grandmother poisoned herself, I'm afraid."

"What?" Sequoia snatched her hand away. "How can you say that?"

"I think you'd better lay it out for us, Harriet," Alex said quietly.

"From what everyone has told me, Alice Haggedorn loved Sequoia like a daughter." She looked at the girl beside her. "You were unusually close to your grandmother, weren't you?"

Sequoia nodded as fresh tears rolled quietly down her cheeks.

"After losing her husband and her son, Sequoia was all the family Alice had left. When her granddaughter became engaged to Terence, Alice began to fear that she was losing Sequoia. She needed something to bind her granddaughter even closer to her. What better way than to develop some sort of unidentified illness?"

When both Sequoia and Alex started to speak Harriet held up her hands. "Wait, hear me out."

She turned her head to look at Alex. "Do you remember when I did that research on nicotine poisoning and I found the two stories about people becoming ill? There was the guy who added nicotine to meat and made a hundred people ill and also the guy who eventually murdered his wife with nicotine. He had given her smaller amounts several times over the prior year to make her sick—sick enough to be hospitalized. His plan was to make everyone assume that she died from the unknown illness."

"And you think Alice did that same research?"

Harriet looked at Fox. "It's certainly possible. I have no proof of course. Alice had months to come up with a plan. I suspect that if you had somebody dig into her home PC you'd find that she had researched various poisons.

"All Alice had to do was find a good set-up to carry out her little scheme. Terence wasn't supposed to come on this trip with Sequoia and Alice—he showed up out of the blue, hoping to get on Alice's good side. Alice planned to poison herself with the nicotine, have Sequoia's undivided attention, and hopefully keep it once they returned to New York."

"I wouldn't have left Gamma. I could have loved her and Terry."

Harriet patted Sequoia's arm. "I know. I'm guessing at what your grandmother was thinking of course, but what I've learned supports my theory. Unfortunately Alice miscalculated. She should have been ill from the nicotine, but would have survived if she hadn't had an allergic reaction to it. I didn't put it together at first but her face was incredibly bloated under the mask when she stumbled into the spa's lobby."

Alex pulled his personal PC from his pocket and flipped through his notes. "Right. Dr. Clarke found elevated levels of histamine in Alice's blood. That was the reason she gave a verdict of severe allergic reaction to nicotine as the cause of death."

He set the PPC on the table and nodded to Harriet. "I think you're on the right track so far. Keep going."

Harriet breathed an inward sigh of relief. Encouraged, she pressed on.

"The morning she died Alice spoke to me in the spa lobby and I misunderstood her. She reached out to me and said 'mis . . . take' and I thought she said 'Miss . . . take'. I thought she wanted me to take her hand, but she was trying to tell me she'd made a mistake. She died before she could get it all out."

"It's a reasonable theory but what do you have to back it up?" Fox asked.

"Earlier today I spoke with the housekeeper who looked after Alice and Sequoia's rooms. Their suite comes with a kitchenette. She told me that she assumed Alice had a nasty drug habit because she'd noticed a number of cigarette filters in her trash Alice's second day here. She noticed because they weren't herbals and she knows real tobacco is prohibitively expensive."

Sequoia shook her head. "Gamma never smoked. She hated the smell."

"I assumed as much." Harriet took a moment to gather her thoughts.

"I think Alice took the tobacco from the cigarettes and soaked them in something to draw out the nicotine, then cooked it down and added that to her mask. The housekeeper said the kitchenette was missing a small saucepan. I'm guessing Alice dumped it in the trash somewhere else on the island when she finished with it."

"She had to carry the nicotine in a container of some kind," Alex put in. "I would have found that among her things or in her treatment room when I searched it."

Harriet turned to look at him. She could almost see his brain working the angles and picturing the scene.

"You're right, there was a container. Alice threw it into the jungle before Nakeesha Bain arrived to give her her massage."

"You found it, didn't you?" The admiration in Alex's eyes was unmistakable.

Harriet nodded and reached into the back pocket of her shorts and pulled out a small, folded pill container that you could buy at any convenience store.

"The hotel lobby store carries these. I searched the jungle floor below Alice's treatment room but the bag had blown away toward the cove and was caught up in some bushes. I'm not positive of course, but the inside smells like nicotine. If you have it tested I think it will show traces."

Alex took the bag and frowned.

"Sorry about my fingerprints. Since Solly and Fox had already been on the ground below Alice's treatment room I didn't really expect to find anything and I wasn't prepared. When I found the bag I was afraid to leave it there in case the wind carried it out to sea." Harriet gave Alex an anxious look.

He shook his head. "You did great. I'm not complaining. I just wish I had solved the case." He smiled then, leaned toward Harriet, and gave her a kiss on the mouth. "Pretty damn smart of you, sweetheart."

Harriet felt the blush creep up her neck to her cheeks. She couldn't believe Alex had kissed her on the lips in front of all these people.

Sequoia suddenly jumped up from her seat, ran around the table, and threw her arms around Leighton. "Can you ever forgive me?" she sobbed.

Leighton pulled her down onto his lap and cradled her. "Shhh. Of course I forgive you. I love you, Sequoia. If you'll still have me, even knowing I'm a failure, I'd like to marry you."

"You're not a failure." Sequoia dashed the tears from her cheeks with her hands. "You're . . . challenged. That's what Gamma always used to say to me when something didn't work out the way I planned. 'Don't give up, Sequoia,' she'd say. 'You can't fail if you never give up.'" She gave Terry a brilliant smile.

"Oh honey. I'm the luckiest man on the planet."

Harriet suddenly felt uncomfortable witnessing what should

have been a very private moment. She stood and tucked her chair under the table.

Alex and Fox stood as well and all three made a hasty departure. Harriet didn't think Sequoia and Leighton even noticed.

"Good work, Harry," Fox said, once they stood on the ground in front of the hotel. He punched her lightly on the shoulder. "You'd make a fine detective."

"Thanks, but I like my job. I think I'll leave the detecting up to you two. Unless you get in a jam again, of course."

Fox laughed and took off.

Harriet watched him go before turning toward Alex. She suddenly felt miserable.

"I guess you don't have to stay with me anymore." She kept her voice light and gestured with her hand. "You know, now that there's no threat." *Please come up with a good reason to stay with me,* she pleaded silently.

A long moment passed before Alex reached out and held Harriet by her upper arms. "Are you in that big of a rush to get rid of me?" he asked softly.

Harriet couldn't speak. Alex's dark gaze was locked on her face. It pulled on her in a way that stole her breath. She could feel the heat pouring off his body, enveloping her. Her flesh beneath his hands burned in a good way.

She locked her knees to keep her legs from wobbling. All she could do was shake her head.

He continued to stare at her until she found her voice. "No. I don't want you to go. I want you to stay with me," she finally managed.

CHAPTER TWENTY-EIGHT

Alex led Harriet to his motorcycle and climbed on. She climbed on behind him and held onto the sides of his tee shirt but he gently grabbed her hands and wrapped them tight around his waist.

"Hold onto me, sweetheart."

Sweetheart. The endearment made Harriet's heart swell. She squeezed Alex tight and laid her cheek against his broad, strong back.

The lights were off in Solly's cottage when they pulled up to Mermaid. Selfishly she hoped her friend wouldn't come over even though she knew the roar of Alex's Triumph would wake him. She slid off the bike and walked toward her front door with Alex's arm around her waist.

They didn't turn on any lights. They didn't speak. Once inside, Alex turned Harriet toward him and kissed her–a long, slow kiss that clearly telegraphed his intent.

"Harriet." He broke off the kiss and leaned his forehead against hers. "Are you sure you want this?"

"Yes. More than I've ever wanted anything."

"Thank god."

Alex swept her up and carried her to the bedroom. She expected him to lay her on the bed but he stood her beside it.

"Wait here. Don't move," he ordered. He crossed the room and threw open the lanai doors, letting in soft moonlight and the perfumed breeze of the tropics at night.

Returning to her, he gathered her in and kissed her again, deepening the kiss and pulling her tight against his heavily aroused body.

It was a heady sensation. Harriet had never experienced pure lust like this with her ex. Bradley had never been able to become aroused with her, something he had always claimed had been her fault.

She had taken on that responsibility, assuming she was too tall, not voluptuous enough, not pretty enough–in essence, not womanly enough for a man to want her.

But pressed against her was the proof that she *was* enough. The knowledge was freeing and made her feel giddy.

"I want to undress you." The words were low and rough and sent a shiver of desire through Harriet's body.

"Yes. Oh yes, Alex, please."

Alex peeled away her clothing slowly, kissing her bare skin as he went until she was trembling with need and could barely stand.

When she told him so he laughed–a low, masculine sound of satisfaction–but he took mercy on her and laid her on the bed on her back. He kissed her long and slow again before moving slowly down to her breasts. Then he proceeded to do wonderful things to her body, to make her feel things she had no idea were possible, until she lay limp and slick with sweat and panting for whatever came next.

The sense of intimacy that she felt when Alex entered her body was enough to make her weep.

"I had no idea. I had no idea it could be like this," she whispered as she wrapped her arms and legs around him and matched his rhythm until they both cried out with release.

Alex lay beside her afterward, his head propped on one hand, and his free hand moving over her body in long, smooth strokes. She felt the strength in that hand, the rough palm of a man who wasn't afraid to work with his hands. She could see his eyes watching her in the moonlight.

"You were a virgin. I thought you lived with your fiancé."

"I did." Harriet hesitated. Until Solly had recently guessed the truth, she was used to hiding the reality of her relationship with Bradley. Searching Alex's face, she knew she needed to share the truth with him. She didn't want lies, even lies of omission, to fester between them.

"We never had sex. Bradley tried but-but he claimed I wasn't womanly enough for him. He couldn't–you know–so he didn't like to touch me."

Alex's hand stilled. "That bastard. Trust me, sweetheart, it wasn't you. That was all on him. You are an incredibly sexy woman." He hesitated. "Was I your first for . . ." he lifted a hand . . "everything?"

Harriet nodded. "Do you mind?" she asked, feeling suddenly anxious. Alex was obviously very experienced in bed while she knew nothing about how to please him. He must have slept with other women who knew exactly what to do for a man.

A slow smile creased Alex's face. "Not only do I not mind, I am touched and honored." He leaned down and took one of her nipples gently between his teeth and flicked his tongue across it.

Harriet moaned but pushed slightly on his shoulder to make him stop. "Teach me how to give you pleasure the way you did me. Please."

"Gladly, but I need some sleep first." Chagrined, Alex realized it was true. He'd been pulsing with need earlier, but he had hit a wall. He needed to recharge, he thought ruefully. Long gone were the days when he could power through several days on only a few hours sleep and then pleasure a woman for hours on end.

"But–"

Alex kissed Harriet's temple and pulled her head down on his shoulder, gathering her close. "I'm not going anywhere, Harriet. We've only just begun."

Harriet snuggled in, marveling at the magic that could happen between two people.

She'd never lusted for Bradley, not really. She knew that now. The feelings she'd had for Bradley paled compared to what she experienced with Alex. What an innocent fool she'd been. All those tears shed because of her ignorance. Believing Bradley's impotence was her fault.

She pushed the memories away, not wanting them to taint the beauty and wonder of the present moment. Bradley was her past. Tonight she had the sexiest man on the island in her bed. Make that the sexiest man she'd ever met. Even Solly rated him a *hubba-hubba* and Solly was an experienced connoisseur of man flesh.

She was head over heels in love with Alex.

That last thought made her eyes pop open. Solly had been right. She could no longer deny it. She loved Alex Hayes. The knowledge made her smile as she drifted to sleep.

They made love twice more, the last time as the pearly rose-gray light of dawn filtered through the lanai doors. Harriet gave as much as she received. The knowledge that she could indeed pleasure Alex filled her with confidence and happiness.

Spent, she lay spooned against Alex's front and watched the world come to life outside her bedroom. Birdsong grew as the island's feathered residents sang the sun over the horizon. With the sunrise came a freshening breeze that stirred the mosquito netting around the bed. It was idyllic. Perfect.

"I love you, Alex. You don't have to feel obligated to love me back, but I wanted you to know how I feel."

Alex's arm tightened around her waist. He kissed the side of her neck. "Are you sure?" he whispered.

His breath felt warm and soft against her cheek. Harriet twisted around so she could look into his eyes. They were so blue–the deep, clear blue of a mountain lake under clear, sunny skies.

She raised her hand to cup his cheek and felt the roughness of a night's beard growth. The intimacy of the touch, of having the right to touch him that way, made her chest feel tight.

"I love you," she repeated. "I'm very sure."

"That's good, because I intend to have it all with you, Harriet. I want marriage and children. A family. And I want it with you. Not right away. But eventually. I love you too."

He kissed her, and poured the love he was feeling into the kiss, then gathered her close again.

They would make a family, but not right away. First they had to deal with the damage that had been inflicted upon Harriet's mind by her aunt. Damage Harriet was still unaware of. They needed to recover her memories of what had to be the worst day of her life and the years that came before. And then he needed to help her deal with those memories.

Alex tightened his hold on Harriet and made a silent promise to be there to help her through it.

For the the first word about releases, sales, news, and special notices, sign up for my newsletter. https://charleymarshbooks. com/mystery-newsletter/

You can find the next book in the series, Frozen in Paradise, at your favorite retailer: https://books2read.com/FrozeninParadise

Turn the page for a preview of the next book in the Destination Death series, *Frozen in Paradise.*

FROZEN IN PARADISE

Harriet Monroe, Public Relations Director for the Island Resort, chided herself for losing track of the time. She was scheduled to meet with the resort's world famous chef Simon LeBrecque . . . ten minutes ago.

She groaned and began to jog slowly along the pink crushed shell road that connected the south end of the island to the north end. It figured that on a day when she needed one of the resort's golf carts that were found *everywhere* for anyone's use there wasn't a single one in sight. Harry ran nearly every day on the beach after work but running in a skirt and moderately heeled sandals was just wrong.

She slowed back down to a walk. There was no point in arriving all hot and sweaty and disheveled. Mr. LeBrecque would not appreciate it. She had called him and apologized for running late and hoped his scowl was for something happening in the kitchen and not directed at her personally.

Despite feeling stressed over her late start Harriet couldn't resist taking the time to appreciate the beauty of the tropical island. She'd arrived three months before and still marveled over how different it was from her native New England.

Sugar fine white sand separated the road from the sun-speckled turquoise water on her left. Lush jungle plants filled with colorful birds, lizards, and insects bordered the road on her right. Large, exotic blossoms perfumed the air and coconut palms soared overhead.

She approached her office but didn't stop, skirting around the pale stone building to the kitchen building behind it. All of the buildings on the resort were built from the same pale limestone and ranged in color from white to soft yellow.

Every building on the island was also built to withstand a Category Five tropical storm. Easily replaced thatching disguised solid concrete roofs that made the buildings strong as bunkers.

No expense had been spared in constructing the resort. Its owner, Douglas Wade, was the wealthiest man on the planet. He was also a recluse. Harriet hoped to meet him one day to thank him for hiring her and for all he'd done for her since.

She pulled open a wide, carved wooden door and entered the kitchen building's small courtyard. Open to the sky, the unusual entry held a round, dark stone fountain with three bronze dolphins arcing out of the top. Water spouted from the creatures' mouths, cascading down several tiered catch-basins. Small peach and green plumed birds flitted in the fountain's middle tier, picking up tiny insects with soft chitters.

Large, perfumed, tropical flowers in brilliant reds, pinks, and yellows grew around the courtyard's edges and three palm trees stretched far above the roof edge. There were several seating areas with cane chairs and small round glass tables for the kitchen staff's breaks. To Harriet's eyes the peaceful courtyard looked like a small zen garden.

While the Island Resort provided over the top luxury for its guests, it didn't neglect the staff who looked after those guests and made sure the place ran smoothly. The staff housing was well above average and working conditions were enviable. She felt incredibly blessed to be working there.

Remembering how late she was, Harriet hurried across the courtyard and through a door opposite. A short, functional, white-tiled corridor led her to the resort's largest kitchen–the strictly-run domain of Chef LeBrecque.

She found the world renowned chef standing in the center of the spotless white tiled room with his arms crossed over his chest, scowling at everyone. Tall and portly, the famous chef wore his silver streaked black hair slicked back into a ponytail. His dark brown eyes darted everywhere and missed nothing.

Chef was master and commander of his domain and his loud baritone voice made sure everyone within shouting distance knew it. Harriet had been intimidated by the chef the only two times they'd met in person.

She sucked in a deep breath and squared her shoulders now as she prepared to confront him for the third time.

"Third time's a charm," she whispered. The man had no power over her, she reminded herself. She had no reason to fear him. They were equals in the employee hierarchy.

Dozens of droids and humans, all dressed in resort-blue double-breasted chef coats and toques, worked at the three long rows of stainless tables that dominated the center of the kitchen. Some chopped vegetables on large wooden cutting boards, some fed freshly made doughs through pasta machines.

In an alcove off to one side a man wrapped in a bloody apron butchered a large meaty leg Harriet couldn't identify on a thick wooden slab. The sight made her feel slightly nauseated and she focused on the droids washing leafy greens at the food-only sinks instead.

The room smelled of yeast and fresh herbs and roasting meat and blood.

A row of industrial dishwashers and several more sinks big and deep enough to hold extra large pots and pans sat against the wall to Harriet's left. One long wall held a row of eight burner gas stoves, six stacked, built-in ovens, and several charcoal grill tops.

An old-fashioned wood-fired oven took up one corner. Wood-fired ovens were rare, found only in exclusive restaurants that could charge enough to cover the cost of the wood fuel since cutting trees for firewood was prohibited worldwide. The wood-fired pizza made here had quickly become one of Harriet's favorite meals.

Several chefs dressed in head chef whites stood before the stoves or barked out orders to the blue-coated staff working at the prep tables.

Two pair of huge stainless doors on the fourth wall lead to the industrial chillers.

To Harriet the scene looked chaotic, but she knew that the flashing knives, leaping flames, and abundance of activity was actually a finely choreographed dance. Chef LeBrecque would accept nothing less.

She stepped into the fray and approached the regal ruler of all she saw.

"Chef. I apologize again for keeping you waiting."

Chef LeBrecque turned his scowl her way. "I don't have time to waste, Ms. Monroe. As you can see I am a very busy man. My constant attention is needed to ensure that every morsel that leaves my kitchen is perfect."

Harriet looked around the kitchen. The staff was hopping, it was true. But Chef was doing nothing more than standing around and terrifying his crew as far as she could tell.

"Of course, Chef." There was no point in arguing. She needed to maintain a civil relationship with the man since she had several publicity ideas for the resort that involved the restaurants.

"This shouldn't take up much of your time," she continued. "I simply want to verify that the ice sculptures for the Pelookie anniversary dinner are correct." She saw LeBrecque stiffen and knew she'd said the wrong thing. Damn temperamental chefs anyway!

"I'm sure they're superb, Chef," she added quickly. "I expect nothing less from you, but I wouldn't be doing my job if I didn't check on them myself. You understand, surely. I'm sure you are the same way with everything that leaves your kitchen."

The chef looked mollified and Harriet breathed a sigh of relief. Coddling temperamental co-workers was not one of her strong suits.

She followed Chef to the left set of stainless chiller doors. He punched in a code which she knew meant that the freezer hadn't been opened yet that morning. The set of doors to the huge walk-in refrigerator were in constant use, but no one had needed anything from the freezer.

That was a good thing as far as Harriet was concerned. The four large ice sculptures for the Pelookie party were fragile and had taken nearly a week to make. If one was damaged there was no time left to replace it. The Pelookie anniversary party was scheduled for that evening.

One hundred family members and close friends had descended on the resort for a week-long celebration culminating with tonight's party. Many of the resort's staff would be happy to see them go. The Pelookies had a tendency to be demanding and autocratic.

An icy blast of air hit Harriet as the chef opened the door, making her shiver. She should have thought to grab a sweater or a jacket, she thought ruefully. Her silk suit that was perfect for the island's mild temperatures offered little protection against the sub-zero temps of the industrial freezer.

A row of LED lights set in the center of the freezer's ceiling snapped on when the door opened, lighting a ghostly fog that formed as soon as the cold air met the warm, moist air of the kitchen.

Stainless steel shelving lined the walls to the left and right.

The shelves were filled with plastic containers and boxes, contents unknown to Harriet. The air had a slightly stale, chemical odor to it.

Chef LeBrecque moved deeper into the freezer with Harriet right behind him. She crossed her arms over her chest, hoping to retain some of her body heat. Damn, it was cold.

"You'll see that I did a superb job on the ice sculptures, Ms. Monroe."

"Call me Harry, please, Chef. Everyone else does." Not realizing that he'd stopped, she bumped into Chef's back.

"Sorry, Chef. I wasn't watching where I was going."

A strangled sound came from the man in front of her.

"Chef? Are you all right?"

Chef turned around and grabbed Harriet's arms. His mouth gaped open and his eyes were wide. "It's-it's–"

"Chef?" Harriet pulled her arms free and stepped around the chef's large body to see what had upset him. Had someone broken one of the ice sculptures?

"Oh no. No, no, no." Harriet shook her head as she reached into her knapsack with trembling hands for her link. It didn't work inside the freezer so she hurried back into the kitchen.

"Alex? I think you'd better come over to the kitchens right away." Harriet turned to look inside the freezer again.

"Come as soon as you can. There's a body in the freezer."

ABOUT THE AUTHOR

In her younger days Charley Marsh's curiosity drove her to climb mountains, canoe rivers, and explore caves and wilderness areas from Maine to California. She's been shot at, caught in a desert flash flood, and almost drowned off the Maine coast. Once she tobogganed down a 5,000+ foot mountain.

Life is always an adventure if you have the right attitude.

Charley never set out to be a storyteller, but looking back on the elaborate lies she made up as a troubled teen she can see that she always had the makings. Now, in the words of Lawrence Block, she happily "makes up lies for fun and profit."

www.ingramcontent.com/pod-product-compliance
Lightning Source LLC
Chambersburg PA
CBHW050408190726
48284CB00007BB/2480